TABBY MONROE

Ghost Track

BLACK CHERRY
PUBLISHING

Contents

Keep in touch with Tabby!

Want to hear about Tabby's latest releases as they come out? Want exclusive sneak peeks, cover reveals, giveaways and other awesome stuff?

Hell yeah you do!   Sign up for Tabby's newsletter here: https://www.tabbymonroe.com/newsletter/

Prologue

⁓⟡⟡⁓

The sun beat down against the back of the man's neck, burning hot on his pale skin. A constant reminder that he was far, far away from the snowy mountains of home.

"We're not in Kansas anymore, Toto," he muttered to his kayak, dragging the boat to the river's edge. Over the rim of baked dirt, steam billowed off the surface of the Boiling River, its milky rapids churning and spitting with heat. Across the desert valley, mountains loomed up on both sides, caging him in here with this furious river and the legions of scorpions and snakes. It was quiet this early in the morning, with the sun barely bleeding over the horizon. Last night's chorus of howls had long faded, leaving him alone with the whispering breeze and bubbling rapids.

He was crazy. It had crossed his mind more than once this morning as he packed up his camp in the blue wash of dawn. He was as reckless and unhinged as the adventure blogs claimed, coming out to one of the world's deadliest rivers seeking...

what? Acclaim? Respect? A rush of adrenaline that was getting harder and harder to come by?

He pushed those thoughts away. They were a distraction, fogging his mind, and he needed to keep a clear head if he wanted to survive the next few weeks. This was no average river expedition, when the worst that could happen to him was drowning or a hungry river beast. Sure, those were still ways he could go, but by coming here, he'd added *boiled alive* and *supernatural creatures* to the list of threats.

No wonder the adventure blogs were railing against him and lauding him by turns. They couldn't get enough of this scheme, pestering him endlessly by phone and email in the build up to Day One. The same websites that published glowing interviews with him followed up with think pieces on his odds of survival. They had his obituary polished up ready to go.

Maybe they were right. Maybe this need in him, this bottomless drive to do more, go faster, beat slimmer and slimmer odds... maybe it was a kind of sickness.

Too late now, either way. Packing up his kayak and carrying it back through the desert, back into the nearest town—it was unthinkable. His career would be ruined, but more than that—he'd never be able to look himself in the eye again.

One more trip. He'd finish this expedition, then he'd take some time off for the first time in years. He'd reflect. Figure out what he wanted; what was coming next.

Maybe it was an ordinary life. A wife and two kids; a house in the suburbs with a white picket fence.

Or maybe it was another trip—something bigger and better even than this. Something audacious. He smirked, checking and double-checking his gear.

Yeah. That sounded more like it.

He'd chosen his entry point to the river after weeks of deliberation. On the one hand, the Boiling River stretched inland for hundreds of miles, traveling through endless desert and winding into the mountain ranges. He could have sought out the source of the river, made an attempt at the whole length of it, but after sleepless nights of research, he'd been forced to admit that was a separate expedition altogether.

No one had kayaked the Boiling River before. He was already smashing boundaries, forcing the adventure community to rethink what was even possible.

So, fine. One step at a time.

In the end, he'd opted for this exact spot: an innocuous bend in the river, deep in the desert valley. He'd chosen it for its shallow banks and slowed rapids, offering a safer entry point. For the promising camping spots at steady intervals along the river. And because from this exact point, the Boiling River left the mountains' embrace and wove out into the desert wastes.

He checked his equipment one last time, running through the checklists in his head. It was second nature to him now, but that was where the danger could slip in. Plenty of talented explorers let themselves relax too much—got cocky and complacent. And when they paid the price for a sloppy gear check or less than vigilant navigation, they paid the ultimate price.

That wouldn't be him. He demanded the best from himself. Top performance. And when he lowered himself into his kayak, securing the spray deck and gripping his paddle, he did so with a clear head and a steady heartbeat.

Just another day at the office. The man leaned forward, sliding off the river bank into the water.

* * *

The river was vicious. Majestic. It fought him and tossed him; it danced with his kayak like the world's weirdest tango. After a few miles, he stopped trying to chart an exact path and let the river carry him where it may. It swept him around bends and spun him in rapids, and rather than fight it, he focused on keeping his kayak upturned.

On an ordinary river, he could dunk under and roll up again. But the Boiling River lived up to its name. Even a foot above the surface, his cheeks prickled with heat and sweat rolled down his temples. His hands were pink and raw where they gripped his paddle, except for the white of his knuckles.

It was painful. Reckless.

It was euphoric.

When he'd pictured the desert, he'd imagined still, baking heat, shivering crickets, and a parched mouth with swollen tongue. This wasn't his first rodeo, after all—he'd done plenty of expeditions in deserts.

This desert, though, had a breeze. Maybe it was the speed of his kayak, racing down the river, or maybe it was the shape of the valley funneling the wind. Either way, warm air rushed past his cheeks, soothing the blistering heat of the river. And as he twisted and lunged, evading death with every move, his face stretched into a grin.

This was it. This was what he came for. This thrill, this heady, floating feeling—this was what he risked his life for, over and over, until everyone called him a madman.

He threw his head back and whooped at the sky.

He didn't grab for the river bank until dusk dulled the landscape, making it harder and harder to see. He heaved himself out of the water with aching arms, his muscles screaming for a gods-damned rest. And when he collapsed onto the dirt, his chest heaving, he watched the magic aurora pulse between the stars with a sloppy smile on his face.

Camp. He'd make camp in a second. He'd light a fire to keep the desert creatures away; he'd burn one of the packs of sage he'd brought to ward off evil spirits. And he'd fix a hot dinner for his grumbling stomach; give his muscles a chance to rest and repair.

They'd need it. Because this was only Day One. Tomorrow, he'd do it all again.

The man laughed, rolling onto his bruised side, and pushed up on wobbly arms.

He couldn't wait.

* * *

It happened on the fifth day. Day Five of the infamous Boiling River Expedition. The man went through his morning routines and checks, eating the planned amount of calories and double checking his gear. He broke camp, locking his supplies in a barrel and stuffing the dry bag into the base of his kayak. And he slid into the milky, simmering water with a calm pulse and his teeth bared.

The river wove further through the desert valley, bringing him past a hotel built high on a ledge. From his kayak, he watched figures bustling past windows; saw lines of laundry flapping in the breeze.

A woman stood on the river shore, her face troubled as she watched him pass. With her long, floaty skirt and layered pendant necklaces, she couldn't have seemed more of a wellness retreat resident if she tried.

He raised a hand in an awkward wave. People were not his

strong suit. Something told him, in the back of his mind, that if they were, he might not be like this.

So extreme. So ready to risk his life. Always chasing after some fleeting, intangible feeling.

The woman lifted a hand in reply, but the frown never left her face. She stood there, staring shamelessly, watching him all the way past until he rounded a bend in the river. Even once she disappeared from view, the back of his neck prickled.

Witches. That must be the witches' hotel. No wonder he was shivering, never mind the heat.

He didn't stop for lunch. Not today. Not when the river urged him on, nipping at his boat, and the memory of the witch followed him for miles. It was probably foolish—the gods knew he needed the calories, and if he lost focus, he'd lose his life.

The man swallowed hard and kept paddling. It was a reckless decision, but it was his to make.

The rock rose out of nowhere. It jutted through the churning rapids, lunging out of a spot that was clear seconds before. The man cursed, digging his paddle into the water and throwing his weight to one side, but the river tossed him like he weighed no more than the bleached animal bones that sometimes bobbed on the current. His paddle caught on something hidden beneath the surface and wrenched from his grip. He barely had time to raise his palms before the river launched him against the rock.

His head slammed back, white lights bursting before his eyes. All sounds faded, and his vision swam. And as the man toppled sideways into the burning water, his last thought was of the witch's frown.

Chapter One

Olivia turned the page of her picture book, smiling down at a dozen sticky faces. Reading Hour was one of the best parts of her job—weaving a spell over the children of Boiling River the way only witches and stories could. Olivia may only be human, but she had her own kind of magic at her fingertips. Magic that could make these kids laugh or gasp or shriek, clinging to each other's arms where they sat cross-legged on the floor.

The library was wrecked, of course. It always was during Reading Hour. The kids blew in here like mini tornadoes, humans and young supernaturals alike, and her beloved library became a wreck of misshelved books and sticky fingerprints.

Puzzles and games were pulled out of the toy boxes and left scattered over the floor. Exhausted parents slumped over the far tables, chatting and sucking down take-out coffees like their lives depended on it. And the children chased each other through the stacks, pulling books out at angles and knocking posters askew.

It was worth it. Olivia didn't mind the clean-up, as long as she got this part: a sea of rapt faces, their tiny mouths hanging open, spellbound by this week's story.

Beside her, on a nearby table, the page of an open book fluttered. It twitched where it lay in the still air, then as she watched out of the corner of her eye, the page trembled upright and flopped over.

Her ghost was getting stronger.

Olivia cleared her throat, pushing all thoughts of the ghost from her mind and making her voice crisp and bright. She read each line slowly, with feeling, taking care to do the voices, and when she reached the last page several kids groaned.

"Read it again!" One boy called out from the back, but Olivia shook her head, smiling.

"You can always ask your mom or dad to borrow it and read it to you!" she sang, placing the picture book down on the table and pushing to her feet. Already, the parents were getting up from their seats, visibly bracing themselves to take charge again.

Something throbbed in Olivia's chest. She should go and see her mom. It had been too long. She'd been putting it off for weeks, guilt churning in her stomach, but now that Bree had seen the ghost's writing too, had confirmed she wasn't going insane—

Tomorrow. She'd go tomorrow.

"They like the stories about pirates the best," she murmured as she cleared up the reading area, her babbling audience flowing back through the stacks. "It's kind of funny. We're so far from the sea."

Maybe it was ridiculous, but since she'd finally confirmed she really was being haunted and not just hearing voices—well, she'd started to chat. Fill her ghost in on the little details of Boiling River. And hey, maybe she would bore him away.

Not that she minded him so much anymore. Now that she knew he was real, he didn't freak her out half so badly. And she could go and see her mom without panic gnawing her insides, without drowning in dread that she was on the same path.

Her mom was unwell. But Olivia... well, it turned out, she just had company.

Unwelcome company, to be sure. But the ghost seemed harmless enough. He recorded her messages on the town's radio broadcasts and wrote her notes in her fogged bathroom mirror. He never tried to hurt her—at least, that she knew of. Over the last few weeks, she'd almost gotten used to him.

He couldn't stay, though. It was *weird*. He saw everything, every moment of her life, and who knew whether he turned his back when she changed? Olivia was a private person. She always had been. So it was time for this ghost to go.

"Here." She waited until the library emptied out, the last family waving goodbye as they stepped through the bright open doorway into the town square's sunshine. Olivia was left in the quiet and shadows, with shivers skating over her skin as her brain screamed that she wasn't alone. "I hope you didn't wear yourself out with that page. This is my only plan."

She laid out a big sheet of drawing paper and an open tub of blue finger paint. The ghost could move pens and pencils, flicking them off tables, but holding them to write seemed a step too far.

Still, he'd traced letters in her mirror. Written *S.O.S* in the fogged window of Otis' cabin. So maybe, just maybe...

Olivia hissed in triumph as the paint dipped, lifted onto an invisible finger. It slid off him quickly, faster than normal, and he hurried to write splotchy letters. *Trapped... in... town. Please... help.* The last word was barely legible, his letters shook so much.

"Well done," Olivia said briskly, screwing the lid back on the finger paints. "Now don't get any mess on the books."

She waited, but there was no reply. No thanks or sarcastic rejoinder. She didn't know why since she'd never spoken with the ghost, but some part of her was sure he was rolling his eyes.

This would work. She chewed her bottom lip as she waited for the paper to dry, drumming her fingers on her elbows. *Bring us something of his,* the witches had told her over the phone. As though it were really that simple.

Well, this would do. It had to. It was his rescue note, after all. And this was Olivia's one and only plan.

* * *

"Spa day!" Bree bellowed across the town square, reaching for the sky. Claire held out her arms as Olivia approached, the roll of paper bearing the ghost's message tucked tightly under one arm.

"This is a rescue mission," Olivia said snippily, pulling Claire close for a hug regardless. Her friend smelled like citrus and turpentine, and even in her day-off clothes, her fingers were stained with dried clay.

Claire was an artist. There was rarely a day when her coppery red hair wasn't splattered with paint. And Bree was now a business owner—ironically one of the most responsible of the three.

You wouldn't tell from her messy dark ponytail or the bikini top poking out of her shirt. Bree barged in for a hug next, squeezing the air out of Olivia's lungs. There were telltale love bites trailing down her neck.

"Ghost first." Olivia held up a finger once Bree let her go, depositing her back on the sidewalk. "Then spa."

Starlight Springs was famous for miles around as a supernatural wellness retreat. As teenagers, the three of them had worn out their day passes, going to steam themselves in the mystic waters.

It had been too long. The memories were almost dreamlike. That was why Olivia had finally caved, agreeing to bring a swimsuit. But this was a rescue mission, first and foremost. She clutched the paper tighter.

The road through the desert was bumpy and wide, and dust kicked up behind the truck as they drove. Bree had borrowed the truck from Otis, her boyfriend and the alpha of the Boiling River werewolf pack. It was ancient and battered, but the engine growled steadily and there were barely any wolf hairs on the seats. Olivia sat in the back, gazing out of the cloudy window, watching the mountains slide past in the distance.

It was funny, growing up in the desert. Just like the kids she read to that morning, she'd never seen the sea in person. Only on videos online, and in documentaries and movies. But somehow, this didn't seem too different. The baked earth undulated, cacti lurching out of the dirt like rocks, and the road shimmered with heat.

She could picture this truck as a boat. The cracks splintering the landscape as ripples.

Ahoy.

The truck lurched over a pothole, and Olivia's gut clenched. She spread the ghost's message over her lap instead, dragging her eyes away from the swaying mountains.

11

He wasn't here. She knew that as well as she knew her own name. After several months, she knew the feel of a room with him in it. She knew the prickle of awareness that spread over her skin when he was near.

Trapped in town. He'd answered her question for her. So that was why he didn't go to the witches himself. She'd wondered and puzzled and wracked her brains about why he was haunting her, of all people. But if he was trapped with her somehow, unable to go free...

Something like disappointment slid through her chest. Maybe he hadn't chosen her after all.

"You look good today," Claire said, craning around in her seat and interrupting Olivia's thoughts. "Like you've gotten some sleep."

"Uh-uh." Olivia smoothed a crease out of the paper. What was she supposed to say to that? *Thanks? Insomnia's a bitch?*

"Have you seen your mom yet?"

"Nope."

"Want me to come with you?"

"I'm good." She was being rude, and she knew it. Her tone was all wrong. Clipped and curt. But her skin was heating, her breaths coming faster, and as the truck bounced again her stomach lurched—

"Okay." Claire gave her a gentle smile, then mercifully changed the subject. "I wonder if they still do palm readings at the Springs."

Olivia latched on to the new topic like a life raft, forcing out comments and questions like she remembered how to be a human being.

Yes, she was sleeping a little better. Yes, she knew now that she wasn't insane.

But something was still needling at her, waking her up in the night and clouding her mind in the day. It wasn't her ghost—he was just sort of there; he hardly bothered her. It was something deeper. Something about her. Something missing in her life.

Maybe the witches could help her, too.

* * *

Starlight Springs sat on a ledge halfway up the valley wall. It clung to the rock face, projecting an odd cluster of lights that shone across the wastes at night. On a Sunday morning, though, the retreat bustled with energy, and Bree circled the makeshift parking lot three times before finding a space. Olivia lurched gratefully out of the truck, pointedly avoiding looking back at the steep, narrow road.

She'd forgotten that part. As teenagers, it barely registered with her that they were driving up a tightrope of a mountain path. She'd been so cocky, so filled with the hubris of adolescence, that it hadn't even occurred to her that they were inches from a terrible fall.

It occurred to her now, alright. Where had that fearless Olivia gone?

"Let's go," she muttered, gripping her rolled paper with damp hands, and Bree and Claire fell into step behind her. Starlight Springs loomed ahead, a sprawling adobe palace with candles burning on every spare windowsill. Ivy and other climbing plants tumbled down the walls, and mosaic tiles were inlaid in the stone, depicting local gods and ancient warriors. The heady smell of incense hung in the air, and somewhere nearby, running water burbled.

Harp music lulled them as they marched up the front path,

interrupted by someone barking orders inside. As Olivia stepped into the lobby, squinting against the sudden gloom, she found a curvy, harried woman standing beside the reception desk, a basket of laundry resting on one hip. Her wild, dark curls were piled on her head, and a few had escaped to dangle over her shoulders.

The woman stopped yelling up the stairs and pasted on a bright smile.

"Hello," she said, voice suddenly serene. "Welcome. Come inside."

"Um." Bree elbowed Olivia in the back, and she stumbled forward, approaching the desk. The paper crinkled in her grip as she held it out to the woman. "Are you a witch?"

Some of the manufactured calm slid off the woman's face, and her canny eyes fixed on the paper.

"I am. Are you a paying guest?"

Bree snorted and elbowed past. She dug her wallet out of her back pocket as she walked, slapping a handful of bills down on the counter. "Three day passes," she told the pink-haired receptionist. The girl—she barely looked their age—jumped and nodded, plucking up the bills with shaky fingers.

Olivia swallowed and forced a smile onto her face. She held the paper out higher.

"Delilah." The witch tugged the paper from her grip, setting her laundry basket down on the marble floor with a thump. "Sun witch."

"Um, th-thank you. Olivia. Librarian."

The smirk the witch shot her was friendlier this time, but it faded to a frown as she rolled out the paper. She traced her fingertips over the ghost's splotchy letters. She held the paper up to the sunlight filtering through the tall windows. Then

Delilah hummed and started to pace, marching back and forth in the lobby.

Olivia backed up to the reception desk, ignoring the hushed murmurs behind her as the receptionist issued three robes and day passes. She watched the witch—Delilah—pace up and down, her fingers curling into tight fists.

"Relax," Claire murmured, making Olivia jump. She nudged her with her shoulder, her freckled face open and warm. "We're in the right place."

Olivia nodded, swallowing down the lump in her throat. She leaned closer to whisper back.

"I feel like I'm in trouble at school."

Claire snorted, the sound echoing around the lobby, and Delilah turned on her heel and strode over.

"What is this?" She thrust the paper toward Olivia, raising a stern eyebrow. "Is this a prank?"

Olivia shook her head, crossing her arms. She wasn't taking back that paper until she had some answers.

"I'm being haunted." She launched into an account of the last few months—the voice she'd heard on the radio; the notes on the mirror; the message. And all while she spoke, Delilah scowled down at the paper like it had personally offended her.

"A ghost didn't write this," the witch snapped, like she'd caught them in a lie. Olivia shrugged helplessly.

"Well, something did."

Delilah hummed again and took up pacing once more, pausing halfway across the tiles to yell at the chandelier.

"Luke! I need you!"

A handsome, dangerous-looking man materialized at the top of the stairs. He strolled down the steps, a graceful hand resting on the banister, and his fluid gait and black tunic made Olivia

15

think of a panther.

"You bellowed, my darling?"

"Look at this." Delilah thrust the paper into his chest. The man smoothed it out, a thoughtful expression settling over his sharp features. "One of yours?"

He shook his head, mouth twisting to one side.

"I rather think not."

"One of… what?" Olivia asked, her voice timid in the cool lobby. She cleared her throat, straightening her shoulders. She wasn't afraid, damn it, and she didn't need to sneak around like a mouse. Olivia raised her chin. "What do you mean, 'one of yours'?"

"Souls," the man said casually, tossing the word at her over his shoulder. He turned back to the paper, tracing the words with his thumb. "Damned souls."

Olivia barely had time to mull that over before the man handed the paper back to Delilah with a shrug.

"This is not the work of a damned soul. I'm sorry, my love."

Delilah grunted, dismissing the man with a wave of her hand, and he winked at Olivia as he sauntered back out of the lobby. She rocked back on her heels, the reception desk digging into her spine, and when the witch said nothing for a full minute, she tossed her hands in the air.

"If he's not a ghost or a damned soul, what else could he—"

"I don't know." Delilah cocked her head, a faint smile tugging her plump lips. "How intriguing." She smacked the paper, the sound making Olivia jump, then gave her a grin. "Enjoy your day at the spa, my dear. Leave this with me."

Chapter Two

*H*e was a loose swarm of atoms, floating in Olivia's kitchen near the bread bin when footsteps bounded up the stairs outside. The key scraped into the lock, the door handle rattling impatiently, and muffled voices hissed at each other through the door.

Interesting. Olivia rarely had visitors.

He pulled himself together by sheer force of will, gathering the remembered pieces of himself one atom at a time. It was harder when she was not around. Her presence anchored him somehow, made him stronger. More resolute. With Olivia on the other side of the door, he had only the fuzzy memories of who he used to be to hold himself intact.

The voices outside the door grew louder, and he sighed as he stood once more on the kitchen tiles. His bare toes grew chilled against the cold floor, and his swim shorts whispered against his skin as he strode into the living room, to the relative warmth of the rug.

"Hello?" The door burst open, spilling three women into the

small apartment. It never felt cramped here when it was just Olivia and him—for starters, he could meld with the furniture if he needed to—but with three grown bodies stomping around, the rooms seemed more cluttered than before. He moved to stand in the middle of the coffee table, watching them swirl around him.

One woman with wild dark hair threw herself bodily onto the squat, plump sofa, scuffing it over the floorboards.

Olivia winced. The others didn't notice, but he did. He noticed everything about her.

"Are you here?" the redhead called, hands planted on her hips by the bookcase. She stared into the corners of the living room, like she might find him there floating in a bed sheet.

"Yes," he told her pointlessly. He always answered. They never heard.

"He's here," Olivia murmured, and his eyebrows shot up his forehead. She could tell when he was near? Could she smell him, hear him, feel him?

But no. She peered into another corner of the room, at the squishy armchair she loved to curl up in to read.

"I missed you." He watched Olivia shoo the brunette off the sofa, the two of them pushing it up against the wall. "I slipped into nothing again." The redhead grabbed one end of the coffee table, dragging it through his legs to the other side of the room, rucking up great folds in the rug as she went. "She won't like that," he told the interloper, jerking his head at Olivia. "She likes things neat."

Sure enough, Olivia darted across the room, kneeling to yank the creases out of the rug. She flipped it back instead, over the top of the coffee table, then the three women stood together and stared at the floorboards. Their chests rose and fell in unison, their cheeks flushed from their redecorating, and a long moment stretched out before the brunette broke the silence.

"So." She dug out her phone, showing the others the screen. "I googled it. This is a pentagram."

"Is there a special way of drawing it?" the redhead mused, cocking her head. "Or do I just copy the image?" Both heads swung toward Olivia.

She pulled out several folded sheets of paper from the pocket of her pinafore dress, smoothing the creases with trembling fingers. He wanted to go to her, to soothe those nerves, but something held him back.

A pentagram. For him.

This could be a good thing. It could be his lucky break. Or his librarian might have finally grown sick of him.

"This is to help me, right?" he called to her, rubbing a palm over his chest. The memory of his heart slammed against his rib cage. "This isn't pest control?"

Because he was a pest. No doubt about it. He'd dogged her every waking minute for months until she'd finally accepted he was real. He'd kept her awake; he'd moved things around; on one especially strong night, he'd flooded her bathroom.

He wasn't proud. He was desperate. No one else had come close to hearing him in Boiling River. To sensing his existence. Only Olivia heard his desperate pleas on the radio, recorded over the town's local jingles. Only her head twitched in his direction sometimes.

"It doesn't say." Olivia turned the paper over, scanning the back. She pushed her glasses up her nose, frowning at the lines of curly handwriting looping over the paper. "It just says draw the pentagram. Then burn the herbs, light the candles, and say the words."

"Right." The redhead clapped her hands together, dropping to her knees. She rummaged in a satchel, producing a piece of white chalk, and crawled to the center of the floorboards. "That's my cue."

* * *

He'd never seen magic done before. Not real magic, with a spell gifted by an actual witch. Sure, back when he had a body and a life, he'd watched videos online and he even went to a magic show once as a kid. He'd traveled through Boiling River on his way... somewhere... and haunted the town since, and you couldn't spend five minutes in Boiling River without seeing something supernatural.

This, though. This was different.

It was occult. Mysterious. Kind of freaky.

"And you're definitely not exorcising me?" he asked Olivia for the third time as he trailed after her around the apartment. It was impossibly more crowded than before, with two men and a woman joining midway through the preparations. One man, a pale vampire with long dark hair, lounged against the wall and watched the backside of the redhead as she bent over drawing with shameless appreciation. The other, a large black man with startling amber eyes, was sniffing around the kitchen counter as the brunette ground herbs with a mortar and pestle.

"It smells like a pizzeria," the man groaned, dipping his face to sniff at the bowl. He dug his phone out of his back pocket, shaking his head. "I can't do it. I'm gonna order."

Whatever was about to happen with the pentagram, it was turning into a sideshow. Olivia's neat, prim apartment was filled with bodies; beers were cracked open and somewhere music was playing. The new woman who'd joined—a short, plump woman with a glossy black bob—sat cross-legged in Olivia's armchair, gnawing on a chocolate bar.

He wanted to shoo them all out. He wanted to pick up their mess, put the furniture back, and smooth the worried crease from Olivia's forehead. She watched the proceedings with her teeth buried in her lip, consulting her sheets of paper endlessly and blinking owlishly around the room from behind her glasses.

"I'll be better," he swore, trying and failing to pluck at her sleeve. His fingers passed straight through the material, through the heat of her arm. "I won't touch the faucets again. Send them away, sweetheart."

This was his home now. The only place he'd felt any smidgen of peace since waking up without his body in the town square. And maybe this spell was to help him or hurt him, but either way, he wanted these people gone.

They were messing up Olivia's stuff. Invading her perfectly organized space. And though she smiled at them, chatting and laughing, he could read the strain in her eyes.

"Go on." He crossed to the vampire, flicking at a long dark lock of hair which had escaped from its tie. The hairs twitched, but the vampire didn't notice. "Get out of here. She's tired, can't you see?"

The vampire lifted a bottle of blood to his lips, his eyes fixed on the artist knelt on the floor.

"Okay." Olivia cleared her throat, her voice strong as it carried through the room. He remembered the first time he'd heard her read to the children in the library—how surprised he'd been that buried in this quiet, reserved girl, there was a deep well of self-assurance.

No one here was surprised, though. They fell quiet, turning to watch her expectantly.

Olivia stood beside the pentagram, nudging a lit candle closer to one of the points with the toe of her ankle boot. She called out a checklist—*candles ready, pentagram ready, herbs ready*—then straightened her shoulders and closed her eyes. When she spoke, her voice was gentle. Almost tender.

"Alright. You need to stand in the pentagram."

It took a moment for him to realize that she was speaking to him. He jerked, stepping back automatically and merging with a lampshade.

"Are you in there?"

"No," he said, voice hoarse. It didn't matter. She couldn't hear him. And so she began to speak, reading from the paper, trusting so absolutely that he'd do as she asked. He lunged forward before she reached the end of the first line, panic clawing at his throat, and skidded to a halt in the center of the floorboards. The candles flared around him, their flames shooting towards the ceiling, and the woman in the armchair sucked in a gasp.

"It's working," the amber-eyed man muttered in the kitchen. The brunette nodded, elbowing him in the ribs.

The words were ancient. Lost words with hidden meanings, their secrets known only to the witches. Olivia squinted as she read them, holding the paper inches from her nose, but whatever the words meant, each landed on him like a blow.

His feet anchored to the floorboards, fusing him in place.

His head snapped back on his neck, his eyes glowing at the ceiling.

And his arms were pulled out to the sides, almost tearing

from their sockets.

He cried out, begging Olivia to stop, but his mouth made no sound. Pins and needles filled him, starting at the soles of his bare feet and surging up, up through his legs and torso and skull, stabbing thousands of tiny points into his faint flesh. Numbness rushed through him in waves, and each time the prickling came back harder, the sensation slicing through to his core. Static crackled through his ears, darkness filled his eyes, and when the pain finally faded, his ears were ringing.

He looked around, chest heaving, sweat slicking his skin.

Six pairs of eyes stared back.

And one pair in particular—icy blue, behind thick-framed glasses—widened as they saw him for the first time. He raised a hand, his limb almost unbearably heavy, and waved.

"Um. Hi."

23

Chapter Three

Olivia blinked at the man in her living room, her mouth as dry as the valley beyond her window. He was here. Standing on her floorboards, the old wood creaking when he shifted his weight. It was the final proof—the final confirmation that she truly had been haunted for the last few months.

This ridiculously handsome man had watched her. Whispered in her ear. He'd seen her eat breakfast every morning; he'd wandered the library stacks as she worked each shift.

He'd written notes to her on the steamed bathroom mirror as she showered. Olivia gulped, flushing scarlet to the roots of her hair.

He was nothing like she'd imagined. She'd pictured... well, a ghost. A blurry figure, almost featureless; a wisp of light curling into form. This man was solid. Broad-chested and toned. His brown hair curled under his ears, and there was a cleft in his square chin.

"Um. Hi." The man raised a hand and waved, moisture

beading on his forehead from the effort. Was he in pain? Did the spell hurt him? She hadn't even stopped to think—

Zacharias spoke, his deep voice baffled. "Why is the ghost wearing swim shorts?"

"He's not a ghost," Olivia murmured, almost to herself. That's what Delilah said, back at Starlight Springs. He wasn't a ghost or a lost soul; he was something entirely other. She stumbled forward a step, reaching out a pale hand, and the man stared at it, nonplussed.

"Do you know where you are?" She schooled her tone, trying to sound gentle. Patient. Abruptly, Olivia wished she'd never allowed the crowd behind her to form. This seemed intimate somehow, a private moment between her and the man who'd haunted her for months.

They had a lot to talk about.

"Your apartment." The man's voice was hoarse. Was that from lack of use? Had he been silent since recording those cries for help on the radio? Or had her spell injured him, made him call out in pain? "In Boiling River."

Olivia nodded, stepping closer and ignoring the murmured conversations behind her. She asked the question that had gnawed at her for weeks, ever since she first suspected she had company and was not simply going insane.

"What's your name?"

The man frowned at the question. He shook his head, as though trying to clear his thoughts. Then he shrugged at her, helpless, his gray eyes clouding with panic, and Olivia whirled on her heel.

"Thank you for helping," she told the others as sweetly as she could manage. "I'll take it from here." Bree groaned and Zacharias muttered something under his breath, but Angie struggled out of the armchair and patted Olivia's arm on her way past.

"Bye, Liv."

"Good luck."

"Bye."

The chorus faded with their reluctant footsteps down the hall. The last thing Olivia heard before her door swung shut was Otis bemoaning the fate of his pizza.

She turned back to the ghost...man...thing. He opened and closed his mouth a few times, searching for words, then stumbled forward, his bare foot kicking a candle. It skidded out of the pentagram, rolling onto its side, the tiny flame flickering out.

The man disappeared. He was gone in the space between breaths. One moment they were reaching for each other, a thousand questions lined up on Olivia's tongue, then she was left staring at the living room wall behind him.

"Shit!" Olivia whirled around, heart racing. Her empty apartment stared back at her, her belongings in disarray. No gray eyes looked back at her; no sturdy, scarred hand reached for her too. "Shit, shit, shit."

"What's wrong?" a voice asked by her ear. Olivia shrieked, jerking away, and the heel of her ankle boot jammed in the gap between floorboards. She toppled, a loud pop sounding from her ankle, and hit the floor hard, palms slapping against the wood.

"Ow." Olivia whimpered, sucking in a shuddering breath before she crawled toward her cell phone tossed on the sofa. She could feel this pain in a second, just a second, once she'd called for help—

Her phone lifted off the sofa cushions, floating toward her. It plummeted towards the ground twice, but each time it wobbled back up, grunts of effort filling her apartment.

"Thanks," she whispered as the phone was pushed into her hand. She called Claire, pressing the phone to her ear and trying not to whimper down the line.

"I'm sorry." The voice was hollow in her other ear. Devastated. "Gods. I'm so sorry. So sorry."

Olivia reached out as she spoke, recounting her fall to Claire, her fingers feeling through the air towards the voice.

There. A slight drop in temperature. A thickness to the air. And beneath her fingertips, cool skin. Olivia hung up the phone, her rescue already on the way, and let her eyes flutter closed. Her ankle throbbed hot in her boot, the pain searing, but that wasn't what she focused on. If she let her fingertips move naturally, without her brain telling them where to go, she could feel the ridge of a jawline, the dip of a chin cleft, the bob of a man's throat—

The apartment door burst open, Claire and Zacharias spilling back through. They gaped at her, crumpled on the floorboards, her pinafore dress creased, and Olivia dropped her hand.

"Hello." She straightened out her skirt. "Um. Yes. Any chance of a ride?"

* * *

"It's not your fault," Olivia whispered as the doctor strapped her leg into a support boot. He shot her an odd look, his movements brisk as he tightened the straps and plucked two crutches from next to the hospital bed.

Olivia didn't care. He could think what he wanted; she wasn't talking to him.

The ghost was here. Her spirit. She could tell.

For the last few months, she was struck several times each day with the feeling that she was being watched. The hairs stood up on her arms; the back of her neck prickled; cold sweat slid down her spine. Olivia would jerk her head around, searching the nearby shadows, scouring all the corners of whatever room she was in, and even when she found no one there, she knew she was not alone.

It felt different now. With the ghost. Spirit. Whatever. She knew he was here by the gentle rhythm of his breath, just on this side of hearing. She could feel the cool patch where he stood in the room; she saw a poster flutter against the wall as he moved past.

He may still be invisible, but Delilah's spell had done *something*. He was stronger.

And now that she'd heard him speak in person, had heard his horrified apologies in her ear, there was no fear in knowing he was close. No sickly, racing heart and lurching stomach.

Just relief. He hadn't gone yet.

The hospital bed creaked as another person's weight settled onto it beside her. The doctor scribbled on his clipboard, oblivious, his back to them both, and Olivia reached out to pat an invisible thigh. The slippery material of swim shorts met her palm, and she choked back a laugh.

This was absurd. Ridiculous. Like something from one of her books.

"Does it hurt?" A man's voice murmured in her ear. She opened her mouth to snipe that yes, of course sprained ankles hurt, but he sounded so freaking miserable that she choked the words back.

"It's not so bad," she lied instead. "Not since the painkillers."

She might as well have popped breath mints, they had so little effect, but she wouldn't tell him that. Not when he sounded so wretchedly guilty.

"Good," the doctor said briskly, spinning to face her. "Be sure to drop off your forms."

Olivia hid a smile as the doctor breezed out, his lab coat flapping in his wake. The ghost cursed quietly, acid dripping from his invisible tongue as he ranted about the doctor's terrible bedside manner.

"Come on." Olivia patted his thigh again. She couldn't help it. He was so firm. "Let's get out of here." She led him through the winding hospital corridors, her crutches squeaking against the linoleum, the fluorescent lights blazing bright overhead. Laminated posters lined the walls, showing cross sections of different creatures' insides.

Human. Fae. Vampire. Troll.

Everyone needed medicine.

"I need something to call you. A name. I keep thinking of you as the ghost, but that's not even right."

A low sigh gusted on her left.

"I don't… remember. I'm sorry."

Olivia chewed her lip, wincing as her ankle throbbed hot with every step. They needed a stopgap. Something temporary, until the man either left or got his memories back.

An image floated through her mind—a movie she'd loved as a kid.

"How about Casper?" Olivia bit her lip, the bubble of a laugh trapped in her chest. Her crutch slid an inch and she hissed in pain, jerking in surprise.

A cool hand steadied her elbow, then passed through her before catching hold again.

"A bit on the nose, perhaps," he said wryly.

"Caspian, then." She'd always liked that name. It reminded her of her favorite fantasy novels—thick, weighty tomes with curling yellow pages and dragons on the cover.

A hum sounded close to her ear. Olivia shivered, gripping her crutches tighter.

"Caspian." He rolled the name around his invisible mouth, drawing out the syllables. "Alright. Yes."

Claire and Zacharias met them in the waiting room, Claire pale with worry and her boyfriend visibly bored. The vampire sat in a low leather chair, flicking at a child's plastic toy on the seat next to him. They both stood as Olivia approached, Claire rushing forward, wringing her hands.

"Is it okay? Are you alright?"

"It's just a sprain." Olivia jerked her head. "Caspian's here too."

"Caspian?" Claire bit her lip, forcing a smile for a patch of empty air. "Nice to meet you, Caspian. I'm Claire."

"Can he hear us?" Zacharias strolled over, his hands shoved in his pockets. Caspian snorted beside her, nudging her gently.

"This vampire likes himself a lot, doesn't he?"

Olivia watched Zacharias carefully, but no scowl creased his forehead. She grinned, a bubble swelling in her chest, even though it made no sense.

It was ridiculous to want Caspian to herself. To want their bond to be special somehow. It would be better for him, for them both, if others could hear him too. If he weren't tethered to her any longer. And yet...

Olivia shrugged, her mood bright despite the horrible throbbing of her ankle.

"He can hear you, but you can't hear him. I guess I'll be

haunted a while longer."

∗ ∗ ∗

It was strange bringing Caspian home. It shouldn't have been—as far as Olivia could tell, he'd basically been living with her for months. Following her from room to room; coming to work with her and for drinks at Silver Bullet.

He knew what her home looked like. Her walnut bookshelves crammed with classics and romance novels would come as no surprise; he knew which artworks she hung on her walls. Impressionist paintings. Soft, beautiful landscapes glowing with buttery sunshine; portraits which spilled over with their makers' yearning.

There was no need to blush and stammer. Caspian already knew she was a hopeless romantic.

"Make yourself comfortable." Olivia's crutches squeaked as she put her weight on them, limping inside the apartment. She glanced around helplessly at her furniture, still pushed haphazardly against the walls. This would keep her up, would bother her all night—she liked things neat, damn it. Perpendicular lines and dusted shelves. She had a whole drawer dedicated to organization tools.

Olivia gusted out a breath. There was nothing for it. She was in no state to drag her furniture back in place, and while Caspian was stronger than before the spell, there was no way he could lug around a sofa.

"We'll figure it out." His voice was soothing, coming from a respectful distance away. "Perhaps your friends could drop in tomorrow and straighten the room. It won't be like this for long."

How did he know it was bothering her? Olivia shot a shaky smile in the direction of his voice, perturbed. He really had been watching her. Making note of her tics and buttons.

"This isn't fair," she blurted, heat rising to her cheeks. "You know so much about me. And yet, for me, you're a stranger."

Caspian hummed. The floorboards creaked under some of his steps, but not others as he approached. This seemed to be the pattern since the spell: he pulsed in and out of solidity, weighing down the hospital bed one moment but then passing his hand through her elbow the next.

"I'd tell you things if I remembered them, I swear." His voice lowered. "I'd confess all my sins."

Olivia coughed, trying in vain to hide the tightening of her throat. This man flustered her without even really being present, and he knew her quirks better than he knew his own name.

Gods, her ankle was sore. Olivia limped to collapse on the sofa.

"What bothers you?" She smoothed out the creases in her skirt. "Something embarrassing, like mine."

"Yours isn't embarrassing." The sofa cushion dipped beside her. "It's perfectly normal. And cute."

Nope. She wouldn't acknowledge that. If she went there, if she let herself feel how alone she was with this handsome, watchful ghost...

"Pay up." Olivia fixed her eyes on the ceiling, on the swirls in the white painted design. "Consider it cost of entry."

"Uh." The sofa creaked as he leaned back. Invisible fingers drummed on the arm. Good. He was mulling it over. "I pretend to sleep sometimes," he said at last. "Even though I can't. Not-not in this form. But I lie down and breathe slowly and act it out like I'm in a play." She heard his gentle huff of breath. "I'd say that's embarrassing."

"It's not." She plucked at a loose thread on the cushion. Once her ankle was better, she'd snip it off. "It's cute," she told him, repeating his own words, her cheeks flaming to life beneath her glasses.

She'd meant it as a joke, but it came out sincere. Good gods, this day was a disaster.

It took way too long, and several grunts, but Olivia wrestled her way off the sofa and back onto her crutches. She limped across the living room, toward her bedroom doorway, and paused.

"Where do you pretend?" She glanced over her shoulder, even though Caspian may not be on the sofa anymore. He could be anywhere. "When you act like you're sleeping. Where do you do it?"

A throat cleared beside her. He sounded awkward. Ashamed.

"I'll stay out here tonight," he told her, dodging the question. It didn't matter. His silence spoke volumes. "I'll pretend on the sofa."

Olivia paused, then nodded. She turned back toward the doorway, limping across the floorboards. As she flicked the living room lights out, the words from one of the picture books she'd read to the children that morning echoed in her mind.

Someone's been sleeping in my bed...

Chapter Four

*C*aspian lied. He did not pretend to sleep that night. Not for long, anyway. Oh, he tried, stretching out over the squashy sofa cushions and marveling at how much stronger the contact felt since the spell. He may still be invisible, may still drift in and out of being, but now he could feel the grain of the cushion fabric, could catch the hint of lavender in the apartment air.

How could he pretend to sleep now? Waste precious minutes and hours of this heightened awareness on feigned unconsciousness? Caspian lay on the sofa, reveling in the molding of the cushions to his spine, for approximately twenty minutes. Then he bounded upright, his bare feet landing with a creak on the varnished floorboards.

He wouldn't snoop. It would be the worst sort of thanks for Olivia letting him stay. Caspian vowed not to rifle through drawers or poke at her mail, even as he strolled around the apartment, hands clasped behind his back.

Something tickled at his brain. Exploration. He liked this

process. It felt right. Natural. Like there was no better way for him to move through the world—even when his world had narrowed to one town, one girl, one apartment.

Caspian began in the kitchen. The effort made him grunt; it sent beads of sweat sliding down his spine, but he pulled open the cupboard doors, his fingers aching where they gripped the small handles. The cupboards were a delicate yellow color, a tasteful addition to the whites and lilacs and natural woods of the rest of the apartment. Olivia's home reminded him of Austen novels and afternoon teas. Vintage dresses and dried wildflowers.

"Here we go," he muttered, craning his neck to read the labels of her tins and packets. This wasn't snooping, he reasoned. It wasn't sensitive information. It was research, more tidbits of information about the girl down the hall to satisfy his never-ending appetite for knowledge of her.

Caspian wouldn't cross any lines. But if this was his world now, he was done sleepwalking through it.

Jarred olives and artichokes. Sun-dried tomatoes and blackcurrant jellies. Olivia's cupboards were neat and orderly, and the cast-iron skillet which rested on her small hob hinted at a person who liked to cook.

Caspian's mouth watered. His stomach clenched on emptiness—on the memory of food.

He'd like to eat Olivia's food one day.

The living room was in such disarray, it didn't seem worth exploring yet. Better to wait until Olivia put it back the way she liked it, arranging the furniture in orderly perpendicular lines. He'd learn more about her that way.

The bathroom was another bust, except for one exception. Her shampoo. It took him what must have been hours, but by focusing all of his newfound strength, Caspian was finally able to flick the shampoo bottle lid open. The scent of violets filled the small room, washing over the white tiles. Caspian sucked in a deep breath, leaning over the claw-foot bathtub, and felt his rib cage expand.

His chest burned. In a good way. This was the best thing he'd ever smelled.

By the time the cool light of dawn spilled through the living room windows, Caspian sat back on the sofa, his head buried in his hands. He'd been given another chance. A new lease on life—or half-life, anyway. And what had he done with it?

Shock Olivia into spraining her ankle. Invade her privacy and pick through her things. And inadvertently confess that he'd been 'sleeping' in her bed for months.

Caspian groaned, rolling his aching shoulders. He may be disembodied, but that was no excuse. It would have been better if Olivia *had* exorcised him, had sent him away once and for all.

He didn't deserve her. Didn't deserve this lifeline.

It was time to go.

An honorable man would wait for her to wake. He'd thank her properly, and assure her he'd never return. Caspian knew that, damn it, but shame was sliding hot and sickly through his gut, and if he looked into the librarian's wide, trusting eyes, he feared the last of his atoms might implode.

Caspian pushed to his feet. There was nothing to pack. No bed to make. He toyed with the idea of trying to leave a note, but even if he could grip the pen, what would he say? He had no forwarding address. No contact details. Only thanks that would never be enough.

The floorboards creaked under his footsteps, still stained with the scuffed chalk outline of a pentagram. Caspian paused in front of the apartment door, glancing back over his shoulder.

Silence. There was no huff of breath; no rustles or signs of waking. Caspian suppressed a rueful smile, swallowing down a lump of regret.

"Goodbye," he told the empty air, voice hushed. "Thank you for everything."

His skin prickled as he passed through the door, the hallway outside already lit with blooming daylight.

Time for Caspian to save himself. And to leave this poor girl alone.

* * *

Boiling River looked different in the first sigh of dawn. It wasn't the quiet streets, with shop fronts shuttered and cafe tables packed away. Over the last few months, Caspian had seen Boiling River at all hours and in all moods.

The difference was him.

Whatever that spell had done, it was like he'd held two bare wires in his hands. New energy, new awareness coursed through his veins, and his senses were keener than they'd been in months. Little details that had faded away for him came back in a rush: bright colors, the spicy scent of the desert, the clatter of the garbage truck making its rounds.

The witches did this. They brought him part way back. And if anyone could complete the process, it was them.

Caspian set out across the town square, the paving stones chilled under his bare feet. Leftover frost from the night glittered in shadowed doorways, and over by the benches a pair of vultures watched him with beady eyes.

Caspian waved at his favorite. The vulture with the bent

feather on its head. Before he'd found Olivia, those birds had been his only friends.

"Wish me luck!" he called. Bent Feather cocked its head and shit on the bench.

Fine. Whatever.

Guilt nipped at his insides as he marched through the streets, leftover shame curdling in his gut, but there was a bounce to Caspian's step too. A swing in his arms. It had been so long since he had hope, since he could *do* something. The new tendrils of control… they were heady.

The florist passed on his right, its huge glass window display filled with artistic succulent wreaths. White and green ivy tumbled from shelves, the leaves tickling at the glass, and a shot of longing burned through his chest.

Olivia. He hoped she would forgive him. Maybe even understand. But he couldn't be a burden to her any longer. Not now, when he had some agency again.

It took three blocks for the bright colors of the shop signs to fade. They dulled to sepia tones, to greys and tans. Caspian swallowed, spinning around and straining his ears.

At the end of the street, the garbage truck drove past. He could see it rumbling, juddering along the tarmac, but no sound reached his ears.

"Shit." Caspian shook his head hard, like he might dislodge a lump of cotton wool. When he strained to listen again, there was nothing.

No whispering breeze. No distant growl of trucks. No rustling insects.

Nothing.

"Okay." Caspian licked his lips. "Okay. They're just sounds. No big deal."

His first step into the desert brought such a strong rush of relief, he nearly crumpled to his knees. This was further than he'd ever gotten since waking up without a body—every time he'd tried to leave Boiling River before, he'd winked out of existence and reemerged in the town square.

Progress. This was progress. Caspian took a second step. And when no invisible forces yanked him back to the town, he stumbled forward, setting off at a run. Starlight Springs was a few miles through the desert, halfway up the valley cliff side.

A rattlesnake shivered in his path, bunching into a tighter coil, its tail shaking soundlessly. Caspian leaped over it, his muscles burning and sweat sliding down his spine, and he couldn't help the whoop which left his mouth. Gods, he hadn't moved in so long, hadn't sweated and ached and fought to keep going—

Black spots filled his vision. Caspian banked to one side, blinking hard and cursing when he bounced off a cactus. His chest heaved from his run, but even as he stood still, eyes clouded, the sounds of his own breaths faded away.

"Shit," Caspian said, and exploded into atoms.

Chapter Five

*O*livia knew the apartment was empty as soon as she opened her eyes. It was too still. Too quiet, too cold. She sat up, her bed covers bunching around her waist, and rubbed a palm over her chest.

It hurt.

Why did she care that Caspian was gone? She'd wished him away a thousand times before. Hell, she went to the witches for that spell specifically to help him leave.

This was a good thing. This was what she'd hoped for, prayed for, calling out to all the local gods big and small to help her ghost on his way.

And now he was gone. Olivia sucked in a wobbly breath. Time to move on with her life.

The morning passed in a blur of burned coffee, creased blouses, wobbly crutches, and misshelved books. Olivia was usually a perfectionist, so fastidious in her work, but no matter how many times she shook herself and gave herself a stern talking to, she couldn't freaking concentrate. Her ankle throbbed in her support boot, never mind the painkillers, and her every thought drifted back to her missing shadow. By the end of her shift, she was ready to pull out her hair.

Was Caspian alright? Did this mean he'd moved on—either found his way back to his body, or passed through the metaphorical veil? Olivia had never particularly bothered with thoughts of the afterlife, but now she found herself lingering in the philosophy section of the Boiling River library, scanning the book spines for answers.

"No, thank you," she muttered, sliding a hardback into place which promised sulfur and brimstone. She was really looking for something hopeful. A book which let her imagine Caspian happy, maybe lounging on a cloud.

"Anybody home?" Bree called from the library entrance, her loud voice bouncing around the stacks. Olivia rolled her eyes, hobbling into view on her crutches.

"It's a library, Bree. You're supposed to be quiet."

Her friend waved her off, stepping further inside. "It doesn't count. I'm not here to read."

Olivia pinched the narrow bridge of her nose. This was such a Monday.

"You do see how that's worse?"

"I brought you these." Bree held up a bunch of grapes. "That's what you do with invalids, right?"

"I'm not an—"

"And this." Bree raised a liquor bottle. It was clear, with a fancy label with hand-drawn flowers. "It's elderflower gin. And my night off from the bar. Figured we could numb the pain Regency style, like those books you love."

Olivia opened her mouth and paused. Her instinct was always to say no, to retreat, to be alone. But now, with Caspian

41

gone and her apartment truly empty... Olivia shuddered.

"Alright," she croaked, limping forward over the tiles. "Give me a minute to lock up. Then you can help me put my furniture back."

"Rock on," Bree said dryly, glancing down at the bottle label. "We're about to get wild."

* * *

Olivia had never been much of a drinker. She liked nice wines, okay yes, and fancy gins. Sometimes, she made cocktails with Claire. But she lacked Bree's commitment to letting loose, preferring to remain buttoned up at all times. The few times in her life that she'd let herself be dragged to Hex Mex, she'd ended up burning the clothes she'd been wearing. They smelled so strongly of spilled beers and cigarette ash and other people's sweat, there'd been nothing for it but a viking funeral.

At least tonight they were in her apartment. In her horribly ghost-less, but now tidied home. Bree had let her direct the furniture around like a conductor, leaning on one crutch and pointing with the other hand. Bree grunted, her forehead beading with sweat, but she dragged the sofa, the coffee table, and the bookshelves around single-handed, her strong thighs flexing in her jeans.

"Thank you," Olivia said primly once they stood in an orderly living room. The rug lay at a perfect ninety-degree angle to the window. She sighed, her chest loosening an inch. "That's been driving me insane."

"Where's the ghostie?" Bree wiped her palms on her jeans, peering into the corners of the room. "Zacharias said you can hear him now."

Olivia cleared her throat. Why did this feel like confessing to a breakup?

"He's gone. I don't know where."

"Oh." Bree eyed her carefully, then marched to the liquor bottle on the kitchen counter. "Mission accomplished! Let's drink."

For once, Olivia agreed.

She wouldn't think about Caspian.

She would not think about her lost ghost. Not even when his absence gnawed at her rib cage and made her breaths come in short gasps. Boiling River was dangerous. He could bump into anything out there, any number of soul-eating creatures. And she'd have no idea! She'd be stuck here wondering like some war widow forever, all because he lacked the manners to say goodbye.

"Where did he go?" she burst out at last, four drinks in. Bree beamed in triumph from where she sprawled on the rug, waving a hand for Olivia to keep going. "He doesn't have a body. He doesn't have a name! Anything could happen to him out there!"

"You might call it ungrateful," Bree suggested casually. She raised an eyebrow, her tongue chasing the end of her straw.

"Yes! Yes. Ungrateful. Like every other human and supernatural deadbeat out there." Olivia sucked in a burning breath, cheeks flushed. "He didn't even say goodbye. Or thank you. Or a single freaking word!"

"Yell it, girl!" Bree toppled back onto her elbow, raising her drink toward the ceiling. Olivia was yelling? "Men." Bree's phone buzzed in the back pocket of her jeans, and she pulled it out to squint at the screen. She huffed, rolling her eyes before barking into the handset. "What? We're having a vital discussion. About how men are useless."

A low voice crackled down the phone. Olivia couldn't make out the words, but she heard the ring of amusement. Otis, then.

Bree's face softened, proving her theory correct. She shot Olivia a glance, her mouth curling into a smile. "Well no, not you. You're the exception, not the rule. Uh-huh."

Olivia turned her face to the side, feigning a retch at her wallpaper. She was happy her best friends had both found love. She wasn't a jealous monster. But did they have to rub it in her face quite so often? Especially now, when her—her *guest* had up and left her without a word?

A chill drifted through the apartment. Olivia shivered, rubbing at her bare arms, goosebumps pebbling over her skin. Her chunky cardigan lay abandoned over the back of the sofa, and she crawled towards it across the floorboards, the room tilting as she moved. Her support boot snagged on the rug, rucking it up behind her.

Gods. Time to switch to water.

"Are you alright?" a quiet voice asked in her ear. Olivia yelped, smacking her elbow on the coffee table. The bone throbbed, and Bree gave her a worried look, holding the phone away from her ear.

"Liv? Are you okay?"

"He's here," she breathed. "Caspian's back."

There was silence beside her. Studied silence, drenched in awkwardness. Bree's eyebrows shot up her forehead, and she hung up the phone with barely a goodbye.

"Is he?" Her lips pursed. "Will he hear me if I tell him he's been a complete asshole?"

"Yes," Caspian muttered beside her. Olivia's heart swooped in her chest.

"He heard you," she said brightly, the room still spinning as she sat back against the sofa. She fumbled for her drink where it rested on the coffee table, the alcohol fumes practically drifting off it like dry ice.

"Maybe you should slow down," Caspian murmured.

Olivia snorted. "Maybe you should kiss my ass." As soon as the words left her mouth, her face flamed scarlet, and she slid two inches toward the floor. Bree tossed her head back and howled with laughter, wiping away a stray tear as she struggled to her feet.

"I'll leave you two to kiss and make up." Olivia flushed impossibly brighter as Bree swiped up her jacket, stumbling on her biker boots. She pointed a stern finger at a patch of empty air by the bookcase. "Make it better, Caspian. Don't make me figure out how to kick your ass. I'm a pacifist."

"Somehow I doubt that," Caspian said as Bree strode to the door. She let herself out with a jaunty wave, and suddenly Olivia was alone in her apartment with an unreliable ghost, a busted ankle, and way too much alcohol in her bloodstream.

"Shit." Was she going to throw up? Could tonight get any more humiliating? Olivia tipped onto her hands and knees and started crawling toward the bathroom. No way was she chancing those stupid crutches right now. Those things were death traps even when she had a clear head.

"I'm sorry." She felt rather than heard Caspian trail after her. He seemed weaker than before, his footsteps silent on the floorboards. Had the spell worn off completely? Could they do it again, or was it a one-use-only kind of deal? "If I could carry you, I would."

Olivia screwed one eye shut, trying to picture the guy she'd seen in the pentagram. His broad shoulders and sculpted chest, tapering to a toned, narrow waist. Yeah, he could probably carry her. You know, if he weren't a wisp of air.

"Who says I'd let you?" she mumbled, wincing as her ankle bounced against the wall.

"I'm sorry," he said again. He sounded hollow. Hopeless. All at once, Olivia's anger drained away, and she paused in the hallway to catch her breath.

"What happened?"

Caspian sighed. "I tried to get to Starlight Springs. I got further than I ever have before, but everything faded once I got into the desert, and then... *poof*. I was back in the town square again."

Olivia's eyes dropped closed. She was being pissy because he left without saying goodbye? Really? Meanwhile Caspian was trying to get his body, his life, his *existence* back. Regret and shame snaked through her gut, and Olivia reached out with a tentative hand.

Cool, sturdy fingers wrapped around hers. Something that was jangling inside her settled.

"We'll figure it out," she promised. "That was only step one."

"Oh?" His voice was teasing. "How many steps are there in the master plan?"

"Difficult to say." Reluctantly, Olivia pulled her hand free and crawled the last few feet to the bathroom. Thank the gods she was such a neat freak; her floors were tidy enough to eat off. Imagine if she had to crawl through Bree's or Claire's homes... Olivia shuddered, nudging the door open. "It's not so much a master plan as a master experiment. This is actually my first ghost rescue, so, you know. There's a learning curve."

"Sure." Caspian pushed the door wider for her. Already, he seemed more solid than a few minutes ago. "It's my first time, too."

The tiles were cold against her palms as Olivia crawled inside the bathroom. All this talk of first times... she steadfastly ignored the heat prickling her cheeks, scrambling up to stand on one leg in front of the sink. She wobbled, hand whipping out to grip the rim, but something steadied her elbow.

The cool water splashed against her cheeks brought her heart rate down. Helped calm her racing thoughts and spinning vision. With her face drenched, Olivia cupped handfuls of tap water, raising them to her mouth to sip.

It was undignified, but who cared? The damage was done. He'd seen her drunk and blushing. And it hardly mattered—by all accounts, he'd slept in her bed for months by now; she'd seen his garish swim shorts.

There was no room for embarrassment between them.

Olivia sighed, tipping forward to rest her forehead against the mirror. She rocked her skull from side to side, grinding her head against the glass, then huffed a sigh and straightened up.

Olivia squeaked. Stood behind her, clear and solid, Caspian blinked back at her in the mirror.

Chapter Six

❧⚬❧

Was that... eye contact? Shock rippled through Caspian's frame. He stared at Olivia in the glass, her wide-eyed gaze holding his.

"Oh my goodness." Her fingers trembled as she reached for the mirror, tracing the side of his reflected face. "I can see you."

"Uh-huh." Caspian swallowed hard, watching his own throat bob up and down. After all this time, all these months of floating through Boiling River, he'd begun to forget what he looked like. Even in his own mind, his outlines had become hazy. The shade of his skin; the color of his eyes; the cut of his hair—they'd all trickled away.

He was tanned. Angular. A pale scar cut through his left eyebrow.

And Olivia looked tiny in front of him, the crown of her head barely reaching his chin. Licking his lip, Caspian raised a hand and settled it on her dainty shoulder. With the visual in front of him, and the feel of her soft blouse under his calloused palm...

Caspian felt more solid than ever.

Olivia cleared her throat, brushing his hand away with a frown. She turned in a wobbly half-circle, flapping her hands to get him to step back.

Caspian saw the exact moment she lost sight of him. Her scowl fixed on a point two inches to his left, and when she hobbled past, she passed through his hip.

"Your crutches—"

"Leave them," Olivia growled. For such a prim, reserved librarian, she had a rock hard core. And as she limped down the hallway, hissing with each half-step on her sprained ankle, a pit yawned open in Caspian's gut.

"You'll make the injury worse."

"Thank you for your opinion."

"At least lean on me—"

"Why?" Olivia snapped. "Are you planning on staying for the next few minutes?"

Right. He deserved that. He'd slunk out of her apartment this morning without a single word. A large part of him was so excited to get to Starlight Springs, to get some answers from the witches once and for all, but it wasn't just that. When he rose from the sofa this morning, it was with Olivia's hiss of pain playing in a loop in his mind. He'd caused her nothing but trouble—haunted her, ruined her sleep, and now busted her ankle, too.

He'd kind of figured she'd be glad to find him gone.

The hunch to her shoulders told him otherwise. It wasn't just the pain of limping down the hallway without her crutches, sprained ankle be damned.

He'd hurt her feelings. Brushed her off like any other stranger.

Gods, he was a wretch.

"I'm sorry I left." His hoarse voice echoed down the hallway. Olivia paused, then continued to the bedroom. Her blouse was creased from sprawling on the rug, her collar curled up on one side. He balled his hands into fists, resisting the urge to reach out and smooth her appearance.

"Why? I'm not your keeper." Olivia barged the bedroom door open with her hip. She threw an irritated glance over her shoulder, skewering an empty patch of wall with her ire.

"It seems like you are, actually. I'm stronger near you."

Olivia huffed. "Lucky me."

"Why do you think—"

"I don't care," Olivia cut him off. She held up a small, pale hand, the fingers so narrow and delicate compared to his. When he saw himself in the mirror... maybe he'd been some kind of laborer? "Ask me tomorrow when I'm not fifty percent gin."

"Right. Sorry." Caspian trailed her toward the bed, hands outstretched in case she tripped and needed steadying. Olivia plopped down on the mattress, smoothing a palm over her patterned bed sheets. Forget-me-not flowers lined the borders, their leaves and stems entwining, and Olivia gusted out a sigh as she picked at the fabric.

The floorboards creaked beneath the rug as he crossed the room. The lamp flicked on easily enough, the strain barely making sweat bead his brow. Caspian turned and did a final sweep of the room before backing to the doorway.

He'd get the crutches here by morning. Somehow. Maybe he could rig some kind of shoelace pulley system, or take the journey in short bursts.

"You can stay." The words were so soft, he almost missed them. Almost passed them off as wishful thinking. But Olivia tipped her chin up, gazing in his direction with her mouth pressed in a firm line. Two spots of color burned high on her cheeks, and a piece of hair was tangled in the frame of her glasses.

"...In the apartment?" Caspian asked carefully. He'd taken more than enough liberties with her. He needed to be doubly sure.

Olivia rolled her eyes. "On the bed. Obviously."

"I don't want to take advantage."

Her snort was very unladylike. He grinned. "It's rather late for that, don't you think?"

"Still." He forced himself to take measured steps back across the room; to not run and leap on the bed like he wanted. "I'm a reformed ghost now. I'm trying to be better."

Olivia tugged the straps of her support boot undone, a faint smile playing at her mouth. She tried to hide it behind the curtain of her hair, but he crouched down in front of her and pressed a ghostly fingertip into one dimple.

"Oh!" Olivia jerked back, surprised, and he gritted his teeth, drawing his strength for long enough to undo her final strap. He slid the clunky boot off her foot, dropping it on the rug, and smoothed his thumbs over her swollen ankle.

She hissed, her foot twitching in his grip, but she didn't pull away. So he rubbed her gently, a frown creasing his forehead, and slowly, the words dropped from his mouth.

"I think... this happened to me before. This injury. Many times, even."

"You remember?" Pale fingers reached toward him, skating over his cheekbone and into his hair. His eyelids fluttered shut for a second, before he gathered himself enough to answer the question.

Concentrate, Caspian. You only get so many chances.

"Not exactly. My mind doesn't remember, but it's like my body does. What I have left of it, anyway. Does-does that make sense?"

"Nope." Her smile soothed the pinch in his chest. "But it's something, right?"

"Yeah." Maybe he *was* a laborer. Or had some other kind of physical job. A welder or a ranch hand or something else that firmed and sculpted his muscles, that dotted his skin with faded scars. "It's a start."

Olivia didn't change into her pajamas. Maybe she was too tired, too tipsy from the gin, or maybe his presence made her self-conscious. He wanted to reassure her, to tell her he freaking loved her cute little sleep sets. The one with blue and cream pinstripes, with a rounded collar and tiny shorts—that was his favorite. He choked the words back.

"Tomorrow will be interesting," Olivia murmured, apparently to herself. She shuffled back along the bed, peeling back the covers to tuck herself in. She looked so small and lost on the big mattress that he rushed to lay down beside her. "A sprained ankle, a hangover, and maybe a runaway ghost."

"I won't run away. I won't leave again, I promise. Not without saying goodbye."

Something flickered across her delicate features, but it was gone as soon as it came. Olivia plucked her glasses off her face and placed them on her bedside table, nudging her journal so that it lay perfectly parallel to the edge.

She paused. "Caspian? Don't read my journal."

"Never." He'd earn her trust somehow. They'd had a crappy start, but he'd make things right with Olivia if it was the last thing he did. "I was never really a reader anyway," he confessed.

"The words always wriggled over the page."

"Dyslexia." Olivia sighed, settling back against the pillows. She pulled the covers all the way up to her pert nose. "You should try audio books."

"I will." He reached out slowly, tucking a stray hair behind her ear. "As soon as I get my body back, I swear."

She smirked, her face smushed by the pillow. "Maybe I'll make you listen to Jane Austen."

"Maybe I'll like it."

Her face softened into a smile.

Yeah. He'd listen to any book for this woman. He'd do anything for her, if only his body would cooperate. Caspian rolled onto his back and stared up at the shadows flickering over the ceiling.

He'd figure this out. He'd find some answers. With Olivia dangling future plans like that...

He was more determined than ever.

* * *

The crutches took two hours and forty-three minutes to bring to the bedroom. Caspian knew, because he kept glancing at the clocks scattered around the apartment.

He was determined to be present. Anchored. And part of that was an awareness of time passing.

It was odd, really. Through all these months of nothingness, he'd been desperate to sink into unawareness. To escape the constant, creeping knowledge that he was here, and no one knew it, and there would be no relief to his loneliness.

He wasn't alone anymore. So Caspian checked the clocks.

Even after the witch's spell, with renewed strength coursing through his limbs, the crutches were still a challenge. They were heavier than they looked and awkwardly shaped—he couldn't just lean his body weight against them and push. Eventually, he settled on the prime technique: pushing the crutches along the floorboards, crawling after them on his knees.

Ancient bruises ached on his legs, and he wondered for the thousandth time who he was and how he earned them. How could he remember so many tiny, inconsequential details, yet forget the biggest thing of all? Every time he felt himself coming close to an answer, his name slipped out of his grasp like a wisp of smoke.

No matter. Caspian grunted, sweat sliding down his spine as he shoved the crutches forward another three inches. He was getting tired again, his hands passing through the metal more often than not, and he tipped back to rest against the hallway wall.

The best rest would be Olivia. To lie beside her and breathe her in. To share the oxygen passing in and out of her lungs; to hover his fingertips over her waist.

He wouldn't do that. Caspian was going to be better.

But his newly remembered morals meant that he wore thin again more easily. He sighed, tipping his head back against the wall and letting his eyes fall closed. The slippery fabric of his swim shorts rustled under his palms as he rubbed his aching legs.

A creature howled on the edge of his hearing. There was the sound of rushing water, pounding over rocks, and the faint smell of sulfur tickled his nose.

Caspian's eyes flew open. The river. He'd known that once, a long time ago. Tomorrow—he'd tell Olivia tomorrow—and in the meantime...

Caspian pushed onto his knees again and heaved at the crutches. They slid another few inches, their lumpy handles catching on the floorboards, and he leaned past to nudge the bedroom door open. Inside, Olivia's quiet breaths swirled the air, and the bed sheets rustled as she moved.

Caspian held his breath and shoved, forcing the crutches over the threshold. They rattled noisily and he froze, his ears straining, but the librarian's breaths were steady and slow. Peaceful.

Good. She'd had too many nights ruined by him.

By the time the crutches lay on the floor beside the bed, his head swam with effort. His body flickered in and out of being, his knee passing straight through the mattress as he climbed back up, and when he lay his head on the pillow, he merged with it up to his nose.

Whatever. Caspian gusted out a sigh, reaching forward subconsciously. He caught himself with his fingertips inches from Olivia's arm, and he balled his hand into a fist.

Nope. He could soak her up from here. He tucked his hands in his armpits and rolled onto his back.

Two hours and forty-three minutes. Not a bad way to pass the time.

Chapter Seven

For as long as Olivia had worked at the library, she had never missed a day of work. The building opened on the stroke of nine AM, and stayed open until every person—human or otherwise—had read their fill.

She ordered in specialty books from across the continent. She organized themed historical displays and pop up art galleries.

The library was her baby. Posting up the 'Closed' sign on the front door hurt her soul.

"I'm sorry," Caspian said for the third time. His voice in her ear made her toes curl. "You really don't have to do this. It can wait until after work."

"We're doing it," Olivia told him, voice firm. She could use the reminder, too. A big part of her wanted to tear that sign down, march inside her library, and get settled behind the desk.

One day. It was one day of missed work. The planet would spin on. And the gods knew how long Caspian had already waited, torn from his body and left helpless in the Boiling River air.

They had a clue now. The river. He'd whispered it to her this morning as soon as her eyes blinked open, as though he'd been scared he'd forget before she woke. But he'd remembered long enough to pass it on, and now it was her job to make it count.

The river… Olivia shuddered as she limped back from the library door. She hated that river. She mistrusted the great outdoors in general, but the Boiling River took matters to extremes. Its scorching heat, its unnerving milky color, the tang of sulfur in the air—she didn't see the draw of it. Yet people came from miles around just to gawp from the riverbank.

A smile tugged Olivia's lips. At least that explained the swim shorts. That was a relief.

When they set off together, her steps painfully slow thanks to her crutches, it was not the river they set off for. Not yet. Olivia led Caspian through the streets of Boiling River, the chill of his presence cool against her arm in the desert sunshine. They passed novelty stores and the fortune teller's tent; the florist and the French bakery. Her crutches squeaked against the sidewalk, the effort of using them making her arms shake, but a cool, invisible arm steadied her elbow and gave her strength.

Olivia sighed when they reached the police station, staring ruefully up the stone steps.

"Perhaps I could try to carry you." A hand slid down her arm. "I'm strongest when I'm touching you, anyway."

Olivia shook her head, chewing on the inside of her cheek. "I'd rather not take the risk. I need at least one working ankle." Digging her phone out of her dress pocket, she dialed and pressed it to her ear. "Danny? I'm outside. Uh-huh."

The cool spot beside her shifted, pacing up and down. Olivia hid a smile.

"Who's Danny?" Caspian blurted, just as the leopard shifter appeared in the station entrance. He strode down the steps, power and grace in every movement. The desert breeze ruffled his wild, tawny hair, and his brown eyes crinkled with amusement. "Oh." Caspian's voice faded to almost nothing, but she still heard his grumble. *"Perfect."*

"Hey, Liv. Been in the wars?" Danny nodded to her support boot. She raised a crutch, giving it a feeble wave.

"You should see the other guy."

"Oh, I bet."

"Is he *flirting*—"

"I need your help," Olivia cut over Caspian. Danny nodded, his hands shoved loosely in his uniform pants pockets, oblivious to the jealous ghost swirling beside him. "It's, um. It's an odd question."

Danny cocked his head. "Try me."

Olivia licked her lips. This had seemed such a solid plan this morning. It made perfect sense as she brushed her teeth. And yet, faced with a real life police officer, doubt and embarrassment tickled her gut.

"If you... um." She cleared her throat. "How would one go about finding a body?"

Danny's eyebrows rocketed to his hairline. "A body? What body?"

Olivia shrugged, helpless. "I don't know yet."

"Liv, if you have knowledge of a crime..." Danny's voice was stern. "Come on. I'll carry you up the steps, and you can make a formal report in my office."

"I don't have knowledge," she blurted, just as Caspian's cold presence crowded at her back. "I have a persistent ghost. Or maybe not a ghost, but some kind of spirit..." she trailed off, shrinking under Danny's doubtful gaze. "He's here right now, actually. If you have questions."

Danny stared at her for a moment, processing her words. His eyes darted to the air around her, passing straight over Caspian's cool patch. Then he shook his head, as though he could dislodge what he'd just heard.

"Come on." Danny pulled away her crutches, handed them to her, and swept her into his arms. Caspian huffed loudly. "Tell me about it inside, and we'll see if I can help."

"Should put in a ramp," Olivia heard a voice mutter as Danny turned and bounded up the steps.

* * *

Danny rested his chin in his hand, scowling at the empty chair beside Olivia. He'd taken it surprisingly well, all things considered.

Then again, Danny was a police officer in Boiling River. He probably heard weirder stories every day when he was getting coffee from the break room.

"The river," Danny repeated. "That's it. That's all you've got?"

"He's wearing swim shorts," Olivia put in helpfully.

Danny sighed, leaning back in his chair. It let out a tortured squeak under his muscled weight.

"Liv, if he's been haunting you for months… there may not be much left to find. The decomposition alone—"

"The witches said he's not dead. Or that he might be alive, anyway. He's not a ghost or a-a damned soul, so maybe it's some kind of curse."

Danny twisted his mouth, face doubtful.

"And he's definitely…" Danny trailed off for a second, then

visibly gathered himself and pushed on. "He's definitely there, Liv? Others have seen him?"

She straightened in her chair, heart pounding. Danny raised his palms, sorrow etched on his face.

"I'm sorry to ask, but with your mother—"

"He's here." Her voice cracked like a whip, and Danny hid a flinch. "Others have seen him. Bree, Claire, Zacharias, Angie, Otis—shall I call them for you?"

"No." Danny scrubbed a hand down his face. "No, I believe you."

She shouldn't bite his head off like this. Wasn't this the exact same fear she'd had for months? She'd denied that Caspian was real for so long, convinced she was going insane—hearing voices like her poor mother.

Danny didn't know that. He was just doing his job. So Olivia forced her bunched shoulders back and fixed her mouth in a smile.

"Good. In fact..." She pushed to her feet, hissing when her ankle throbbed in complaint. "Do you have a mirror? Maybe you can see him too."

Danny paused, then nodded, pushing his chair back. "Wait here."

His footsteps faded down the corridor.

"Does it hurt?" Caspian murmured as Olivia lowered herself back into her seat. "Can I help?" His fingertips brushed over her forearm. Bringing her hand down on top of his, she held him to his skin.

He was real. Solid. The reminder soothed her racing heart.

"I feel like a crazy lady," she whispered, just for his ears.

"You're not crazy." He sounded adorably affronted. "You're helping me when no one else could."

Her thumb rubbed over his knuckles. The skin was ridged with scars, and when she flipped his hand over to touch his palm, she found calluses.

"You worked with your hands," she said faintly. Gods, why did she sound so strangled? It was one embarrassment after another. She may not be able to see him right now, but the physical reminder of Caspian's size—that he was bigger and broader, so solid at times...

Olivia gulped. Danny shoved the door open and she snatched her hand back.

"Here you go." The mirror he gave her was cloudy and splotched with mascara. It folded open in a battered plastic case, clearly meant to fit in a handbag. She peeled it open and angled it at Caspian, smiling in relief when she met his warm gaze.

"You try." She passed it back to Danny. "I already know what he looks like."

Danny plucked the battered mirror from her grip, doubt etched across his face. But when he angled the smeared glass towards the empty chair, his brown eyes grew wide.

"By the gods." Danny stared at the mirror. He tilted it to see all of Caspian, from his bare feet to the top of his head. And when he looked at Olivia, something tightened his expression. "I know him, Liv. I've seen him before."

A cold hand snatched for hers, and she squeezed back.

"You know who he is?"

Danny nodded sadly. "I do."

* * *

The Caspian looking back at her from Danny's computer screen was nothing like her ghost. His mouth was twisted in a cocky grin, his eyes bright, but there was a hardness to his face. In the photo, he shouldered a huge backpack, with a camera slung around his neck.

He was tanned. Vibrant. Kind of sweaty-looking. He looked like the sort of man who could build fires and whittle wood.

"An explorer," Olivia murmured. That explained it. His hard muscles and scarred hands; the damp hairline and blotchy t-shirt in the photo. Caspian looked like the embodiment of the great outdoors, and Olivia had never felt more distant from him.

What must he think of her, with her reading armchair and her complete lack of exercise? She was a homebody; a library mouse. She liked pretty dresses and quiet nights in. Gods, he must have been so bored to have to haunt her.

There was no way he'd have chosen her. That newfound knowledge formed a lump in her throat.

"Jackson Firth," Danny supplied. "Record breaker and all-round jock."

"Nice," Caspian muttered beside her. No, not Caspian—*Jackson*.

Olivia didn't want to be bitter, but gods, she hated that name.

"And what happened to Jackson?" It was sour in her mouth.

"He went missing on a trip down the Boiling River." Danny swiveled the monitor so she could read it better. "Almost a year ago. A witness saw him pass by Starlight Springs, but nothing after that. His gear washed up a few weeks later." Danny shook his head. "It was an insane thing to even try, Liv. The papers said he had a death wish."

"Clearly not," a voice muttered. She ignored it, leaning closer to the screen.

"Was there a map? Any spots where his remains might have washed up?"

"Oh, so I'm *definitely* dead now—"

"Shut up, Jackson." A headache pounded in her temples. Olivia sucked in a breath.

"Caspian," he whispered. "Call me Caspian."

That really shouldn't have made her feel better.

Danny clicked his tongue, drumming on his desk. "Well, there's only one route. Follow the river. We could trawl the banks, check in the caves. We ran a few searches when he first disappeared, but I guess we could have missed something."

"Okay." Olivia sat back in her chair. She squared her shoulders. "That's what we'll do. We'll find his body, and then he can..."

Can what?

"Well. Something will happen," she finished lamely. Maybe he needed to be buried to find peace. Maybe he was held captive somewhere in a magical coma. Whatever it was, they'd deal with it one step at a time.

Then she could go back to her normal life. Alone.

Chapter Eight

꧁ꕥ꧂

The police officers walked in a line, patches of desert stretching out between them. They moved slowly, heads bent, the toes of their boots kicking up dust. Ahead of them, rattlesnakes slithered under boulders and into holes in the dirt. Scorpions scuttled for shelter.

This was really happening.

Caspian stood by Olivia's side, his throat so tight he could barely speak. He should be helping—should join the line scanning the dirt—but something held him back. A cold wash of fear.

It was funny. He'd clearly lived a daring life, smashing records and laughing in the face of danger. And now, when he was beyond the risk of harm, he couldn't bring himself to march forward. To look for his own body.

As if she could sense the clammy nerves breaking over his skin, Olivia leaned her shoulder against his. Her warmth washed through him, never mind her long-sleeved t-shirt, and he took a steadying breath.

"It will be alright," she murmured. Everything about her had been quiet since Danny's office. She barely glanced in his direction, even when he knew she could feel him moving around. Ever since she saw that picture of him on the computer screen, she'd retreated inside. The only place he couldn't follow.

Caspian cleared his throat. "What if I don't want to be found after all? Haunting you isn't so bad."

Olivia snorted—the first sign of amusement in hours. Caspian leaned harder against her, his fingers plucking at the hem of her top.

"There's no guarantee you're safe where you are." She rested her temple on the nub of his shoulder. "If you're alive, you might not stay that way for long. And if you're dead..."

She trailed off. There wasn't much to say, really. Caspian tilted his head down, rubbing his chin in her soft hair. She sighed and melted against him, all her weight on her good leg, and for a moment everything was perfect. If he could freeze time, this was where he would freeze it.

A few feet away, Danny's radio crackled to life. It buzzed against his hip, the words fuzzy, but Danny yanked the radio off his belt and barked fresh orders into the mouthpiece.

"Did you understand that?" Caspian murmured into Olivia's hair. She shook her head.

"I think it's like doctors' handwriting. You have to be in the know."

"Alright, you two." Danny strode over, his mouth pressed in a firm line. Foreboding shivered down Caspian's spine. "There's a cave we didn't check last time. It didn't—it *doesn't*—make sense for him to be there, with the river currents moving how they do."

"Okay." Olivia peered up at the officer. Strong, tall, handsome

Officer Danny. Caspian rolled his eyes. "What about it?"

Danny sighed. Then he fixed his gaze an inch to the right of Caspian's face.

"They think they've found something. Liv, he's there."

* * *

Caspian stumbled almost as much as Olivia as they picked their way across the desert. She pushed forward on her crutches, wobbling on the uneven terrain, but Caspian steadied her from one side and Danny from the other.

Caspian couldn't find it in himself to be jealous. Not even with Danny's sturdy grip on her elbow.

He didn't feel anything. He was numb.

Officers shouted to each other, waving arms and barking into their radios, but the sounds filtered to him from a distance. Everything was warped and muffled, like he was underwater, and the only sound he heard loud and clear was the thumping of his own heart.

Danny didn't say whether his body was alive. What kind of state it was in. He sealed his mouth shut and led them both across the desert.

The path they followed wound between cacti and boulders; dipped through ditches and lurched up steep banks. Danny lifted Olivia over the hardest parts, but she always murmured to be let down again. Her eyes darted in his direction, her concern slicing through his chest, so he watched his feet instead.

This was it. What he'd wanted, what he'd worked for all these months.

So why did it feel like he was walking to the gallows?

"Mind yourself." Danny nudged a huge, hairy spider with his

66

boot. It was unclear exactly who he was talking to—Caspian, Olivia or the spider—but when they reached the edge of the river bank, Danny planted himself closest to the water.

He needn't have worried. Olivia was no reckless fool—not like Caspian had once been. She stayed well back from the riverbank, leaning over and wrinkling her nose at the sulfuric waft of the water. The milky rapids frothed and churned, steam billowing towards the blazing sky, and sweat burst over Caspian's forehead.

The memories came to him in flashes. Pushing off from the bank; sliding into the water in his kayak. The way the river tossed and spun him like a leaf. The rock surging out of the rapids—

Caspian clutched his head, stifling a groan. Olivia reached out for him at once, a crutch dangling from her forearm.

"Caspian? What is it?"

"I remember," he told her hoarsely. "Not all of it, but... flashes..."

Sickness twisted in his gut and he doubled over, catching his breath. Danny waited, sturdy and patient, while Caspian sucked in deep breaths, Olivia's fingers playing in his overgrown hair.

No wonder Danny was a police officer. He was unshakable. For the first time, Caspian was truly glad he was here. He'd take good care of Olivia, if... if...

"Let's go." Caspian straightened up, wiping his arm over his upper lip. "Let's get this over with."

* * *

The cave was cratered. Moon-like. They reached it via a

tangled thread of a path, sawing up and down the riverbank. As they passed closer and closer to the boiling water below, Caspian was actually glad when Olivia quietly asked Danny to carry her the rest of the way. It was one less worry screaming in his brain. He'd never forgive himself if she got hurt trying to help find his stupid body.

A cave. A *cave*. It had really been here all this time?

In truth, although finding out what had happened to him had been his mission all this time, a big part of Caspian never expected it to actually work. He steadied himself with a palm against the damp riverbank. Beads of condensation from the rising steam tracked dusty lines down the rock.

"Easy," Danny muttered, apparently to himself. He walked slowly, watching where he put each foot, no sign of strain on his face from carrying Olivia in his arms. This was everything her beloved romance novels cried out for, but it wasn't Danny that she was looking at. Her eyes darted over the path behind them, following Caspian's hand-prints on the rock-face.

"I'm here," he called out, just for her ears. A relieved smile flashed over her face, before the strain settled back in.

He knew that strain. The same nerves gnawed at his rib cage and tightened his throat.

What if he was dead? What if he had to move on, away from Olivia?

He wasn't ready.

With the first step inside the cave, the roar of the Boiling River faded away. In here, there was only the *plink, plink* of dripping water, and the rustle of sleeping bats overhead. Sharp columns of rock reached out of the ground like fingers, and dangled perilously from the cave roof. The terracotta tinge of the rock gave the cave a golden glow.

Light filtered in. It spilled in glittering shafts through holes in the cave roof, dust motes spinning in its path.

And far in the depths of the cave, it shone through a crack in the ground.

This light was different. It was so bright, it hurt to look at, and when Caspian closed his eyes, it still danced across his eyelids. It burst out of a fissure in the cave floor, dazzling and pure, interrupted only by an object slumped over the crack.

Not an object. A body. Him.

Caspian lurched forward, his steps uneven, Danny striding not far behind. His ears rang as he approached and the body grew clearer—his own limbs, arranged neatly, his face turned up to the cave roof. His expression was peaceful, like he was sleeping, and his chest rose and fell with each breath.

Alive. He was alive. Caspian swallowed a strangled cry.

But even with the joy coursing through his veins, Caspian's steps stuttered. Something was... off. The body's muscles hadn't wasted at all, even after lying still for months. His skin was more flawless than it had been in years. Perhaps it was the golden light, washing over his back and filtering up through his limbs, but he seemed...

Caspian grunted. There was magic at work in this cave.

Danny came to the same conclusion, calling out as his arms bound tighter around Olivia.

"Careful! There's something in this cave. Something super-natural."

With effort, Caspian tore his eyes away from the body and walked back to Danny's side. At the edge of the cave, a police officer's radio crackled as they spooled out crime scene tape.

"Tell him I look weird. Better than before I got hurt. Please."

Olivia relayed the message, her face tense. She patted Danny's shoulder and he lowered her to the ground, his nostrils flaring as he scanned the cave.

"It doesn't make sense," he muttered to himself, then strode off toward the entrance. Olivia was silent, fumbling her crutches back into place. Caspian moved closer without really thinking.

It was automatic. Her presence soothed him. And apparently the feeling was mutual, because when his arm brushed against hers, she sagged with relief.

"This is good, right?" she whispered. She jerked her head at the body. "You're alive. That means there's hope."

Hope for what? That he could stay? In Boiling River, with her? The questions lined up on his tongue, but he swallowed them down.

This was not the moment to bombard her. He wouldn't pressure her when the stakes were so high. Caspian would get that body back, and repossess it, and then he'd make himself worth wanting before he offered to stay.

After all—what did he have to offer her right now? Past fame and a body in a coma? She was smart and beautiful, and she'd read every book under the sun. He struggled to read a page of handwriting.

Olivia blinked up at him, waiting for an answer. Caspian cleared his throat and spoke, mouth dry.

"Yes. It's good. Thank you, Olivia."

Her cheeks pinked.

"This was all Danny."

"No." He leaned further into her warmth. "It was you."

They stood together as the cops bustled around, taking photos and gathering evidence. Two doctors in protective jumpsuits that made them look like astronauts entered the cave and approached the body. They knelt at its side, taking measurements of the light with handheld devices. Then they spread a stretcher over the rock beside the fissure.

"Here we go." Caspian stared so hard, he forgot to blink. The doctors took hold of him under the legs and shoulders, counted to three, and slid his body onto the stretcher.

For a beat, nothing happened. The light swirled out of the fissure, now uninterrupted, and the body lay silent on the stretcher.

Then, as everyone held their breath, the body changed. Scars bloomed over the flawless skin, shiny and red—the burns from falling in the river. A gash opened up above one eye, and an arm broke with a sickening crack. Bruises swelled and puffed up from under the skin, and the clothes on the body shredded.

The breaths raising the chest became shallow. Stilted. Blood pooled on the floor of the cave.

"That's not good," Caspian said dryly, winding an arm around Olivia's shoulders. She trembled beneath his grip. "Look away, sweetheart."

Olivia turned and buried her nose in his cool chest.

The doctors called for Danny, rushing to stem the bleeding, and Caspian watched it all over her head. He didn't look away until the body was carried through the cave entrance, the stretcher sagging between the harried doctors.

"It's over," he promised, pressing his lips against her hair.

Hopefully not for good.

Chapter Nine

꧁꧂

Olivia hated hospitals. When her mother got ill, she spent years of her life sitting in uncomfortable plastic chairs and staring down pale gray corridors.

She hated the incessant beeps of machines. The gurgle of the waiting room water cooler. The buzz and flicker of fluorescent lights. The squeak of cheap, scuffed linoleum under harried feet.

At least when she came here for her ankle, she knew it was in-and-out. Arrive, get strapped and bandaged, and get back out into the spicy desert air. But Caspian…

His body showed no signs of waking.

"Am I lined up right?"

Olivia angled the stainless steel bedpan at the hospital bed. Danny craned over her shoulder, watching the warped reflection too as Caspian lay down in his own battered body.

"Your left arm needs to tuck in." Caspian wriggled into place.

"Try matching your breaths," Danny suggested. For a long moment, there was only one Caspian in the room, his chest rising and falling in shallow gasps. His face was scarred, swollen with cuts and bruises, but the machines he was hooked up to beeped steadily.

"Is that it?" Olivia whispered. "Is he in?"

"No," said a sour voice on the bed. Caspian sat up, levering out of his body at the waist. Olivia watched him in the bedpan, mouth pursed, as he tried to line up his limbs again and lay back.

Danny sighed. "I'm sorry, Liv. I need to go. That cave is... there are a lot of unanswered questions. Call me if anything changes?"

She nodded, turning to wrap the leopard shifter in a hug. She was glad he was here. She'd known Danny for years—had gone to school around the same time—and she couldn't imagine dealing with this with a stranger.

"Thank you," she croaked. "You're the reason we got this far."

"We're not done yet," Danny said firmly. He squeezed her shoulder. "One step at a time."

When his footsteps echoed down the hospital hallway, they were left alone. Olivia dropped the bed pan on to a trolley, limping over to the bed.

"I'm so sorry, Caspian."

An invisible hand wrapped around her wrist, a thumb skating over her pulse point.

"Why? This is progress."

"But look at you." Olivia's chin wobbled as she took in the battered body. "You look like you've been thrown off a cliff."

"I made my choices," Caspian said quietly. "Don't worry about that now."

Olivia scoffed. "That's like ordering someone not to be sad."

"I got lucky." His voice was firm. "That light preserved me

73

somehow. It kept me alive for months, sweetheart. There's no room for regret."

That light... There were plenty of miracles in Boiling River. Phenomena. Inexplicable circumstances. The local art gallery owner had a self portrait which aged for him; there was a time slip by the police station bike racks. Hell, there was more than one fissure in the earth of the desert, and sometimes at night you could hear the wail of escaping souls.

This was no weirder, really. Not for Boiling River.

It still made Olivia's chest cave in.

"Maybe the witches can help," she whispered. "Or maybe..." she trailed off. It was too ridiculous.

"What?" Something rustled as Caspian sat up, amusement brightening his voice. "Are you blushing?"

"It's stupid."

"Well now I have to hear it."

"In movies..." Olivia screwed her eyes shut behind her glasses. Was she really going to say this out loud? "Have you seen any Disney movies, Caspian? Do you remember them?"

He barked a laugh. "You mean when true love's kiss magically brings back the sleeping princess—"

"Shut up."

He laughed harder. Olivia flung an elbow in his direction.

"Shut up. It's been a long day. My ankle hurts. I read too much. And I'm tired."

He trailed off into a chuckle. "No, I like it. Let's try."

"No way. Not when you're such an ass."

A scandalized gasp came from the bed.

"An ass? I am literally wounded, Olivia."

"Assholes don't get healing kisses," she said primly. "I'm sorry, I don't make the rules." She fumbled for the handles of her crutches, a curtain of her blonde hair sweeping forward to hide her flaming cheeks. Her vintage tea dress was creased and streaked with dirt, while her knuckles were scraped from bashing against the riverbank wall.

"Try it." Caspian smoothed a palm over her hair, his voice low. "For science. Go on."

Olivia frowned down at the battered face on the pillow. Caspian's bottom lip was split.

"I don't know. It might hurt you."

"No tongue, then. Rein yourself in."

"Shut up." Olivia smacked at the air, and Caspian caught her hand with a smoky chuckle.

"Try," he murmured, suddenly close to her ear. She shivered. "I want to see."

Alright. Olivia tugged her hands free. She cleared her throat, turning to the face on the pillow. Did she have coffee breath? Would he taste it through his coma? She tucked her hair behind her ears and nudged her glasses up her nose.

"Don't make fun of me," she warned. "And don't be weird. Don't critique."

"I promise," he said solemnly.

Olivia leaned closer to the man on the bed. It was ridiculous, but he felt like a stranger. She knew that square jaw, that cleft in his chin, the curl of his brown hair under his ears. She traced her fingertips down his throat, circling his Adam's apple, and a low sound came from the bed.

Bolder, she cupped the side of Caspian's face, careful of the scars and bruises.

"Wake up, asshole," she whispered, her breath gusting over his lips, then dipped her head and pressed her mouth against his.

There were no showers of confetti. No triumphant brass band. Only the steady beep of the machines, unaffected. Caspian's lips were warm but unmoving, and Olivia straightened up with a shudder.

She scrubbed at her mouth. "Now I feel like a creep."

"Don't," said a gravelly voice behind her. Then firm hands gripped her hips and spun her around. Caspian's chill washed over her, and she arched up against his chest without thinking. He groaned, the noise rumbling through where their bodies met, and she wound her arms around his invisible neck. Her fingers played in the soft ends of his hair; they rubbed against his scalp.

"Why couldn't you do this?" she gasped, biting her lip as he crowded closer.

"I'm doing it now," he said, and brought his mouth down on hers.

Now *this* was a kiss. Olivia's heart slammed against her rib cage as she tugged him closer, the chill of him everywhere. He sent goosebumps scattering over her skin; he made her breasts tighten under her dress. Caspian's mouth moved against hers, cool but determined, and he only flickered out of being twice.

Finally, he broke off with a groan, his forehead dropping to her shoulder.

"If I could," he told her raggedly, "I'd pick you up and kiss you senseless against that wall."

"Just kiss?" Olivia asked in a daze. Caspian groaned, the sound broken.

"Don't. We'll traumatize the nurses."

They weren't the only ones, Olivia thought, her mind scrambled. How was she supposed to recover from this? And how could she admit the most awful truth out loud—that maybe she didn't

76

want to help Caspian after all?

The man in the bed was a stranger. He was warm. All wrong. She wanted her ghost to stay.

* * *

The shower spray beat against Olivia's back, easing the knots in her shoulders. Walking with crutches was hard, damn it. She was one big aching muscle, and today's foray across the desert had only added to the throb of her ankle. Reddish brown dirt clung to her skin in a fine layer, and she'd somehow come home with cactus scratches over her legs.

"Gods damn it," she muttered, closing her eyes and breathing in the lavender scent of her shampoo. The foam ran down her body, picking up dirt and staining beige on its journey to the plughole.

She waited until the water ran clear, leaning heavily on the bathroom tiles. Then she lowered herself, as creaky and sore as a pensioner, to sit in her claw foot tub.

"I deserve this," Olivia told the faucet as she ran her bath. Deliciously warm water spilled over her legs, soothing her screaming muscles. A slug of bath foam tinted the water pink and covered the surface in a thick mound of bubbles.

She lay back. Rested her head on the edge of the tub. Tried to calm the gnawing worries in her chest.

A gentle knock sounded on the bathroom door, and she sat up with a splash.

"Thank the gods," she said quietly, then louder: "You can come in! I'm hidden by bubbles."

"More's the pity." Caspian's footsteps echoed on the tiles. He sounded in a strangely good mood for someone who'd just found his own battered body.

Olivia drew her knees up to her chest, the water sloshing at her sides. This bath tub was the reason she chose this apartment. She could forgive a lot—the low ceilings, the scuffed floorboards, the cursed amulet she'd found under the sink—for this sturdy, gorgeous tub.

She'd treated it right. Lined the room with candles; placed pots of tumbling ivy on the shelves. Usually, when she wasn't being haunted by a sexy ghost, she put music or audio-books on during her baths.

She hadn't today. It seemed rude.

"It's too bad you can't get in," she said without thinking, then immediately flushed red. "Your body looked pretty sore in the hospital," she mumbled. "That's all."

"Uh-huh." Damn him, she could hear his grin. "Plus I'd flood your apartment."

"Again."

"Shit, yeah. I forgot about that. Again."

Olivia rolled her eyes, hiding a smirk as she rested her chin on her knees. Was this such a terrible existence? Sure, he was invisible, and trapped in Boiling River, and only she could hear him...

She swallowed hard. She couldn't do it. It wasn't fair. She wouldn't ask him to stay.

The brush of his fingertips against her cheek stilled her. She was warm, flushed, both with embarrassment and the rising heat of the water. The chill of Caspian's touch thrilled down her spine; it made her nipples pebble against her thighs.

Olivia closed her eyes and leaned into his touch. He rubbed across her cheekbone into her hair; he scratched her scalp gently before trailing down her throat.

"You're not so stealthy," she murmured as she watched the bubbles shift. They parted in the path of his hand, drawing a trail down the center of her chest.

"I'm not trying to be." Caspian slid to one side, skating his thumb over her nipple. Olivia gasped, arching her back, and his answering hiss of breath sent the top layer of bubbles flying.

"How's your ankle?" he asked quietly, switching to her other nipple. Olivia groaned.

"Not the time," she gritted out between her teeth. The icy cold of his touch, surrounded by the molten heat of the bath... her toes curled against the porcelain. His hand roamed over her skin, so callused and broad, cupping her breast then sliding down her torso to squeeze her waist.

"One day I'll do this without having to concentrate." Caspian circled her belly button with the tip of his finger. "Without flickering out like bad WiFi."

"I'll hold you to that." Olivia stared at the burnished brass faucet as Caspian's probing touch slid lower toward the spot between her legs. She licked her lips; she barely remembered to blink. With him invisible, she might as well be blindfolded, but if she squinted at the reflections in the faucet, she could almost see—

Caspian slid up to a knuckle inside her. Olivia bucked her hips, gripping the sides of the tub, and sending a wave of scented water onto the tiles.

"Sorry," she gasped. "Don't stop. Sorry."

"It's okay." He crooked his finger, sliding deeper, and brought his mouth to her ear. "I'm wearing swim shorts."

"Oh, gods." She tipped her head to the side, leaning on his invisible shoulder. "That feels really good, Caspian. Don't ruin it."

He snorted, working his cool fingers in and out of her, rubbing at a spot deep inside. His thumb swiped over her clit and she bit her lip, turning her face into the chill of his neck.

"Have you done this before?" he asked, voice rough.

"By the gods, Caspian," she spluttered. "I'm a librarian. Not a nun."

It was ridiculous, and a half smile was etched over her face as she panted, but somehow their banter drove her higher. It filled her chest with a warm, gooey sensation, even as her legs spasmed and thrashed in the water. He stroked her steadily, his shoulder vibrating under her cheek from the effort of staying solid. And when he pushed her over the edge, her thighs clenching around his cool wrist, she bit down on his shoulder to muffle her cries.

"Ow," Caspian said when she detached her teeth and collapsed back against the tub. The bathroom floor was awash with bubbles, and his presence in the water had turned the water lukewarm.

It didn't matter. None of it mattered. It was so, so worth it. Her limbs were languid and heavy, her muscles relaxed for the first time in days, and her skin tingled from Caspian's touch.

"A few teeth marks are the least of your worries." She turned her head in his direction and smiled. And when his lips pressed against hers, she cupped his jaw and kissed him back with every ounce of the love weighing down her chest.

Chapter Ten

The witch could not have seemed more out of place in the hospital if she tried. She breezed down the sterile, gray corridors, her brightly colored shawls flapping behind her. A waft of incense lingered in her trail, and her sandals slapped against the linoleum. She was curvy and tall—powerful in stature—and more than one doctor cringed out of her path.

A man walked half a step behind, hands tucked in his pockets, his gait fluid and his tunic midnight black. His mouth curled up in faint amusement at the posters lining the hospital walls: faded diagrams and calls for residents to eat their vegetables, use a condom, and take iron supplements between donating blood to vampires.

"Is this her?" Caspian murmured as he and Olivia stood in the waiting room, watching the couple approach. "Who's that man?"

Olivia shrugged. "Luke, or something. Liam. Larry."

"He doesn't look like a Larry."

Though the witch led the way down the corridor, power crackled in waves over the man strolling behind her. It washed over Caspian's invisible skin; it stood his hair on end and made his teeth ache.

"She's the witch, anyway," Olivia muttered, raising a hand in an awkward wave. Her crutches clattered against the floor when she lowered her arm, and the witch swept her with a curious glance as she came to a stop in the waiting room.

"Is this the work of your ghost?" She gestured at Olivia's sprained ankle in its support boot. "Want me to banish him to another realm?"

"No," Olivia said quickly, even though the witch was right. Her injury was his fault. All of this was his fault. "I slipped at home. It's nothing. Cas-Caspian's through here."

She was nervous. Olivia only stuttered like that when she was on edge. Caspian waited until the couple strode into his hospital room before running his palm down her back. She sighed, the muscles relaxing a fraction beneath his hand. When she began to limp forward, he tugged her back by the blouse, speaking urgently into her ear.

"We don't have to do this. I promise, sweetheart. I'm happy with the way things are—"

Olivia's eyes swam as she glanced at him, her mouth lifting in a wobbly smile.

"Come on, Cas. We've found your body. You're still alive. We can't stop now."

"But—"

"Come on." She pulled away, her crutches squeaking as she limped through the door. Caspian paused, his heart lodged in his throat, his heart racing inside his chest. He should feel happy, excited—anything but the gnawing panic and foreboding he felt right now. Muffled voices inside the room jolted him forward, and he followed through the doorway.

The room was crammed with machines and bodies, the blinds on the window fracturing the morning sunshine. The witch—Delilah, Olivia had called her—stood on the other side of the hospital bed, peering down at his battered face with detached curiosity. The man in black waited nearby, lounging back against the windowsill, while Olivia squeezed in next to the machines to take Caspian's hand where it rested on the bed. Her small, pale fingers wound through his own blunt, scarred ones, and something kicked in Caspian's chest.

He was jealous. Of himself.

Gods, he was a wreck.

Delilah clicked her tongue as she prodded his body's arm. She pressed her fingertips to the pulse point in his throat; she traced a sigil over his forehead and flipped his hand over to read his palm. As she inspected his physical form in the bed, Olivia told her in a halting voice about how they'd found him.

The cave. The light shining through his flawless body. The injuries that bloomed over him when they took him away.

Delilah didn't twitch an eyebrow. This cave was not new information, then. The man behind her even looked bored, tilting his chin back and watching a spider knitting a web across the ceiling.

"You say he fell into the river?" Olivia nodded, biting her lip. Delilah glanced at her, a faint line creasing her forehead. "Then how did he find himself deep inside a cave, moving against the currents?"

Olivia's mouth moved, but no sound came out. She nudged her glasses up her nose, then finally said: "Danny said something about that. Um, the police officer. He said it didn't make sense."

Delilah hummed. "Of course it makes sense. With the right information."

The man pushed away from the windowsill, joining the witch beside the bed in three languid strides. He tucked one of her wild, dark curls behind her ear, his fingertip lingering on her throat.

"Shall we begin, darling? I made us brunch reservations."

Delilah snorted. "Gods forbid that I keep you from your bacon."

The man's eyes crinkled in amusement, and they shared such a tender, fleeting glance that even Caspian's chilled body flushed hot for an instant.

"He's here, I suppose?" Delilah asked, breaking the man's gaze to look at Olivia. "Your ghost. He's ready and willing?"

"Yes," Olivia whispered. She squeezed his body's hand tighter. "He's here."

"Alright." The witch flapped a hand, forcing the man to step back and give her space. "Open the blinds. Let in the sunlight. Let's begin."

* * *

Caspian had always been a cynic about magic. Oh, he knew it existed—he wasn't a complete fool—but when it came to his own life, he preferred to put his faith in his own abilities. The mystic arts were just that: arts. Subjective and flighty. Hard to predict and control. Only a desperate man would submit his fate to them.

Well, he was desperate. Caspian hopped up onto the hospital bed, relieved to hear the mattress groan beneath his weight.

The stronger he was, the more solid, surely the better his chances were of this working. He lined up with his sleeping body, aligning his feet and ankles first, then moving up the legs and torso.

"Am I in?" He darted a glance at Olivia. She had her back turned, the smudgy pocket mirror she'd started carrying around held over her head. She squinted into the glass, tilting it to check from the top of his head to toes.

"Yes. Um." She cleared her throat as the man rounded the bed and peered over her shoulder, stooping to look at the reflection. Caspian raised a hand, waving at the man, and his dark eyebrows twitched.

"Interesting. A living soul." He spoke casually, like they were two birdwatchers who'd spotted an oddity. "We don't get many of those."

"We?" Olivia asked. "Who's we?" The man smiled down at her, power crackling off him and flickering the lights.

"Figure of speech, my dear."

Delilah ignored them all, striking a match and holding the flame to a handful of sage. She waved it over the length of his body, muttering under her breath, the acrid smell tickling his nose.

"He must have been knocked loose somehow."

"You make it sound like losing a tooth."

The man shrugged. "It's not so different."

"Oh." Olivia angled the mirror at the pillow. "I think he hit a rock in the river."

The man hummed. "That might do it. Yes, the river is more magical than not. And if he'd angered it somehow—"

"If you two don't mind," Delilah ground out, eyeing them across Caspian's body. "This is a complex, fiddly ritual. If you

85

can't be quiet, you'll have to wait in the hall."

"Sorry, Delilah," Olivia whispered, cheeks burning. The man smirked, eyes glittering with dark promise as he feigned zipping his mouth closed. Caspian shifted on the mattress, throat dry.

"This might pinch," the witch warned him, her fingers spread six inches above his face. He nodded, even though she couldn't see him, and forced his limbs to lie still as she began to speak.

They were ancient words. Lost words. The same language that Olivia had read off the scrap of paper during the first ritual, but this time spoken with confidence. Fluency. Delilah's voice dropped an octave, her pupils dilating as she spoke until her eyes were fully black. The sunlight shone brighter through the window, filling the room with bright, golden light, and a low hum began on the edge of his hearing.

Caspian sucked in a breath. It sliced his throat on the way in, rattling around his chest before gusting out again. His heart slowed, its thump sickly and weak, and in an instant, his skin stretched tight and raw. It hurt, but he couldn't grit out a moan, couldn't even open his eyes. The room was dark, light flickering behind his eyelids, and his bones were battered beneath his bruised flesh. Sickness surged in his gut, bile rising up his throat, and the humming grew louder now, rattling his teeth in his jaw—

"What's happening?" a woman's voice asked by his side. "It's hurting him!" Someone squeezed his hand, cool fingers gripping his own. And even that tiny contact was agony, pressing into his raw, ruined skin—

He arched his back, eyes rolling back in his head. Distantly, beyond the fevered twitching of his muscles and the buzzing drone of voices in his head, he heard the crash of furniture. The grip on his hand was snatched away. He levered his jaw open, driven for some reason to reassure, to say that he was alright, even as his tendons wound so tight they nearly snapped. But no words formed, and after an eternity, he crashed back down against the mattress.

There was stillness. Silence. The comforting embrace of nothing.

Then, one by one, his senses faded back. First, there was the blistering ache in his body, the pain that rippled through him with every clench of his heartbeat. He tasted blood and bile in his mouth; he smelled musty river water and the sharp tang of antiseptic. The steady beep of machinery nudged at his brain, along with low, muffled voices, and bright light shone through his closed eyelids.

He didn't know how long he lay there, focusing on the painful draw of each breath. Maybe two minutes. Maybe two hours. But when he finally forced his eyes open, the effort sending beads of sweat sliding down his forehead, he found three pairs of eyes staring back. He darted a glance around the room, taking in the monitors and stainless steel trolley. The walls and floor were pale gray, and golden sunshine spilled through the blinds.

A hospital, then. That explained the pain. And the smell, and the beep of the monitors.

A large woman with huge dark curls cleared her throat. She was draped in layers of jewel-toned shawls, with amulets hanging around her neck and rings on every finger.

"Caspian?" the woman asked. He swallowed hard, head spinning. Caspian?

"I..." His voice was hoarse with lack of use. It grated on his throat, and he licked his dry lips. The woman turned and plucked a cup of water off his bedside. "Thanks," he managed, then lay there helplessly. He needed to sit up, but the thought of gathering his strength, of pushing onto his elbows—

Click. His bed began to hum, rising up at the waist and doing the work for him. A man with dark hair and golden brown skin stood behind the woman with the water, his finger pressed on a remote control on the sheets.

The man caught his eye and winked. The room span again.

A small hand gripped his fingers on his other side, and he turned his head on the pillow. Another woman stood over him, this one with icy blonde hair and thick-rimmed glasses. She chewed on her bottom lip, her gaze raking over the length of his body beneath the sheet.

He cleared his throat and nudged his hand free. Stricken, the woman stepped back. Something clenched in his chest, but he couldn't examine it now. There were too many questions swirling around his head, too much to absorb.

He turned back to the woman with the water. Took the cup with a trembling hand. And asked his first questions.

"Where am I? What happened?" He glanced quickly at the blonde woman. "And who are you?"

Chapter Eleven

*T*wo weeks later, Olivia sat in the Silver Bullet bar, wincing as she moved her ankle in a circle. She'd handed back the crutches and support boot with relish, but somehow in the last few weeks, she'd forgotten how to walk and stand like a normal person. Her awkward gait, the swooping sensation in her gut every time her ankle wobbled on the sidewalk, and the dull leftover aches put her in a vile mood.

Yeah. That was the problem. Her leg.

Olivia scowled and knocked back her bottle.

"Liv?" Bree's head poked around the doorway which led to Bree's apartment above the bar. The Silver Bullet was her baby—the business that she nurtured with endless love and patience—and it was rare for an evening to pass without Bree coming down to check on things.

"Hello." Olivia lifted a heavy arm, wobbling on her bar stool. She stifled a burp. "You found me."

"... Yeah." Bree stepped fully into the bar, locking the door

89

behind her. She wove between groups of after-work drinkers, dodging pool cues and boisterous arms. When she came to a halt in front of Olivia's stool, she squeezed her shoulder, a frown etched on her forehead. "You'll need to hide better next time."

"Noted." Olivia rested her head on the bar. If she closed her eyes, the raucous sounds of the drinkers and the jukebox blurred together and faded. It was almost peaceful.

"Okay." Bree tugged her upright, grabbing her chin to check her eyes. "Do I need to cut you off?"

"I'm not drunk." It was true, no matter how bitter she sounded. She may feel heavy and sluggish, buried deep in her thoughts, but it wasn't an alcohol-induced melancholy. This was her first drink, and she'd barely downed half of it. She didn't even like beer.

"Then why are you draped over my bar?"

"I'm just…" Why was she here, again? "My apartment is too quiet."

"Ah."

No. No, no. She didn't come here for pity.

"Not 'ah'," Olivia snapped. "There's no 'ah'. There's nothing wrong, I'm just trying something new. Trying to support your stupid business."

Bree snorted, spinning the beer bottle to read the label.

"Is that right? Could have bought a nicer brand, then."

"I'm a librarian, not a billionaire."

"Shame. I need some work done on my bike."

Olivia huffed a laugh, a reluctant smile tugging her lips. She may resent the pity, but in truth, this was exactly what she came here for. The company of someone who knew her, and a distraction from the yawning pit in her chest.

Caspian was gone. Not just returned to his body, but *gone*. Like he never existed. And now his body was walking around Boiling River, mocking her with every glimpse she caught.

"Have you spoken to him?" Bree asked gently, the question interrupting her thoughts.

Had she spoken to him? In a sense. When he first woke, she'd exchanged a few awkward sentences with the man in the hospital bed. She'd taken him flowers after a couple of days, along with a bunch of grapes. And a week later, when he was discharged from the hospital, she'd bumped in to him in the Boiling River town square.

She'd opened her mouth, a thousand words lined up on her tongue, but he'd given her a polite smile and nod, then walked past like she was no one.

She'd stood there, rooted to the ground, hunched over like he'd kicked her in the chest.

It didn't matter. Olivia didn't want to speak to him. She wanted Caspian, not Jackson Firth. Rugged explorer; distant stranger.

Please.

"Why is he still here?" she grumbled, ignoring Bree's question. "He must have people he needs to get back to. Family or friends or whatever. You'd think Boiling River would be the last place he'd want to stay—"

She broke off, spinning on her stool when the bar door chimed open. A group of three demons walked in, flicking their hair out of their eyes and grinning at the giggling tourist girls. Olivia turned back to the bar, ignoring the disappointment sinking through her gut.

"Danny asked him to stick around." Bree cocked her head, but Olivia smoothed her features, even as hurt licked at her insides. Apparently some small part of her had still hoped that she was the reason he lingered in town. "It's still an open investigation. You know what Danny gets like. He's obsessed with that freaking cave."

"Really? There are way weirder things in the desert."

"Try telling him that."

Olivia swigged from her bottle, not sure what else to say. The taste made her nose wrinkle, and she placed it back on the bar with a thump.

Bree's hand squeezed her shoulder again, her grip almost as strong and callused as Caspian's had been.

"It'll be okay, Liv."

"I know." She shot her friend a wry smile. "How can I miss what I never had?"

* * *

"Thanks for this, Liv." Danny clapped her on the shoulder, his quick eyes already scanning the landscape. The desert was cool, washed blue by the pale light of dawn, and only the occasional rustle hinted at its creatures.

A shadow passed over. A vulture wheeled overhead, its wings stretched wide.

"No problem," Olivia mumbled. And it *was* no problem—it wasn't like she slept properly these days, anyway. She'd been up hours before she needed to leave her apartment. And it wasn't like she could refuse Danny this favor, not after everything he'd done for her and Caspian.

"Shall we?" She arranged her face into a smile. Danny raised an eyebrow, unconvinced.

"In a second. Jackson's joining us."

Olivia swallowed, her mouth suddenly dry. Perfect. When Danny called her late last night, asking for her to retrace their path to the cave with him, she'd assumed it would be just them.

"Why do you need me here, again?" Olivia coughed. She sounded strangled.

Danny frowned at her before shading his eyes and scanning the valley. "Jackson doesn't remember anything from before he woke up. You might notice something he doesn't."

This cave. This gods-damned cave.

Who cared how Jackson had survived?

Danny was convinced he had help somehow, but even if he did, so what? It was hardly a crime, saving someone's life. Olivia dug the toe of her hiking boot into the dirt. The morning breeze tickled her bare legs below her shorts, and she tugged them lower, suddenly self-conscious.

If she'd known Jackson was coming, she'd have... what? Dressed up? Dragged a brush through her hair, rather than throw it up in a messy bun?

Pathetic. It didn't matter what he thought of her. He was a stranger, after all.

A stranger who had kissed her. Touched her, his fingers tracing down her stomach into her bathwater, delving between her legs—

"Here we go," Danny said, shattering her thoughts. Olivia sucked in a steadying breath and turned to offer the approaching man a polite smile.

He looked tired. Still covered in scars and scrapes, with dark bruises below his eyes. It was surreal, seeing him in jeans and a white t-shirt instead of those freaking swim shorts.

She missed them, Olivia realized, manic laughter bubbling inside her chest. Gods. She was insane.

Caspian—*Jackson* smiled in return, his gaze lingering on her. Olivia looked down at her boots. They were stiff and new, straight out of the box. A dead giveaway that she was no explorer.

"We'll start here." Danny clapped his hands together and rubbed them. "We walked this way last time," he explained to the other man. "We'll head to the river, then along the bank to the cave."

"And what are we looking for, exactly?"

Jackson's voice was rough. Like he still hadn't smoothed the edges off it since waking up.

Didn't he have anyone to talk to? Someone he could call at home? Olivia chewed on the inside of her cheek, staring out at the mountains.

"Anything." Danny shrugged. "Everything. Whatever might trigger your memories or give us a clue."

"Because you think I had help."

"I think you had help." Danny nodded and shot Olivia a brisk smile. "Shall we?"

When Olivia agreed to this morning hike, she'd pictured an easy chat with Danny and a chance to stretch her legs. Maybe work her tender ankle a bit; get some sunshine and fresh air on her cheeks.

She had not imagined this. Jackson falling into step by her side. He adjusted his stride easily, slowing to match her steps, and somehow that tiny gesture made her chest ache.

It wasn't him. Wasn't Caspian. But she still itched to reach for his hand. She glared at her feet instead, watching her step, concentrating on the hiss of rattlesnakes and the crunch of dried bones under her boots.

"How's your foot?" he asked, so distant and polite.

Olivia snorted. "Just fine. How's your whole body?"

"Uh. It's okay."

She didn't know this man, she reminded herself for the thousandth time. She couldn't prod him like Caspian, couldn't expect the same reactions. But then Jackson leaned down, his breath tickling her ear.

It was so familiar. So *Caspian* that tears stung her eyes and air rattled in her chest.

"I've never been good in the desert," he murmured. Like he was telling her a secret. "I'm a snow guy."

Olivia shot him a look. "Weird choice of trip."

Jackson shrugged, straightening up again. He stepped easily over a bleached cattle skull, regardless of his words.

"It's not exploring if you only go someplace familiar."

She wouldn't know about that. The furthest Olivia had ever gone was about three towns over. Her friends were here, her library, her mom—truth be told, it never occurred to her to leave. Not when she traveled every time she cracked open her favorite books.

Danny saved her from outing herself as a homebody. He called over from a nearby boulder, and Jackson went to go look. Olivia glanced too, but it was a lump of rock. To her, it was the same as any other. Just like these cacti all looked the same, and she couldn't tell one bend in the Boiling River from the next.

"Anything?" Danny asked them both, hope lightening his brow. When they both shook their heads, his shoulders slumped, but he kept walking.

They were here to prod at Jackson's memories, but as they neared the river, it was her palms that grew clammy. Olivia wiped them on her shorts, stumbling to keep up, trying not to think about the steam billowing off the water in twisting columns.

He fell in that water. It scarred his beautiful face, left his skin shiny and raw. Yet Jackson studied the river, unperturbed, while Olivia gasped for breath behind them.

It must have hurt him so badly. And they put Caspian back in that body, made him feel those injuries again—

"Liv?" She blinked hard, coming back to herself. Danny stood in front of her, ducking his head to meet her eyes. He frowned, his mouth tight with concern, but it was Jackson's expression that made her heart clench.

He stared at her over Danny's shoulder, his gaze so intense it burned hotter than the river. He searched every inch of her face, his lips parting slightly, and his chest shuddered as he took a deep breath.

Then Jackson looked away, turning back to the river, his hands shoved in his pockets like nothing happened.

"I'm fine," she mumbled, brushing Danny off. "Just tired. Let's get on with it."

Chapter Twelve

What was with this girl? The Boiling River librarian. Olivia. Somehow, he'd made an enemy while in a coma.

She said his name like it tasted bad in her mouth. Hissed the 's' in Jackson, like she thought him no better than the coiled rattlesnakes sunning themselves out in the desert. Yet he caught her staring at him so often, he'd started to recognize the feeling, his hair prickling on the back of his neck. But when he looked back at her, she turned quickly away, her pale blue eyes shuttering.

She made it perfectly clear with her hard eyes and pursed mouth: she wanted nothing to do with him. Gone were the shy smiles and stilted questions from her visit to him in the hospital, a bunch of grapes and bouquet of flowers clutched in both hands. Somewhere between that awkward visit and this morning hike, he'd fallen out of her good graces.

Shit.

It really shouldn't bother him this much.

She was nothing to him—a stranger—and yet her silent dismissal made his skin bead with sweat. Jackson brushed it off, swiping his forehead on his arm and striding deeper into the cave.

They were here for a purpose. To find answers to the police officer's questions.

Not so this tiny librarian could make him feel like crap. And he'd been nothing but polite to her, thanking her for the grapes and forcing himself to make small talk.

He'd tried, damn it. She had no right to judge him.

The cool, damp air of the cave was a relief after the baking desert. Truly, what was he thinking when he came here? There were more than enough ways for him to risk his life in colder climes. He could prove himself anywhere in the world, and yet he'd dragged his pale, overheated ass to this desert valley in the armpit of nowhere.

He'd leave soon, Jackson decided. The moment this cop was done with him, he'd leave this town and never look back. The thought cheered him, and he picked his way across the uneven rock with lighter steps.

Something scraped across the ground, the sound echoing around the cave walls. Jackson froze, straining to listen, but he could only hear the rustling of bats overhead and the rasp of his own breath. He turned, cocking an eyebrow at the police officer five steps behind. The man was a shifter, after all—some kind of big cat. He'd heard the nurses whispering when the cop left his hospital room.

They needn't gossip. It was clear from the officer's smooth, rolling gait; from the power and grace simmering beneath his toned muscles. If Jackson could do that—if he could shift into an apex predator at will—there was no challenge on earth that could best him.

But then it wouldn't count, of course. The records were only worth beating when they nearly beat him first.

The officer—Danny—nodded, pressing a finger to his lips. He tugged his uniform shirt clean over his head, shoulders flexing, and over by the cave's mouth, Olivia's eyes widened behind her glasses.

Jackson swallowed, fighting the bizarre urge to stride over to her and clap his hand over her eyes. It was nothing to him if the librarian had a crush on Danny—he certainly shouldn't want to scoop her up and carry her away over his shoulder.

Gods. Jackson scrubbed a hand over his jaw, the tightness in his chest easing as Danny's leopard form loped past toward the scraping noise.

It was the head injury. That must be it. He'd whacked his head on that river rock and lost some of his good sense in the process.

With Danny gone, it was harder to remember what he was doing here. Jogging memories, he knew, was the general idea, but how did you deliberately jog a memory? Jackson wandered around the cave, breathing in deep lungfuls of musty air and concentrating on the distant rush of the river. Maybe something would tickle the hidden recesses of his brain.

"Anything?" Olivia asked by his shoulder. Jackson jolted, nearly stumbling into a rock pile. She was quiet when she moved, never mind those stiff, shiny hiking boots. Must be a library thing.

"Uh." He cleared his throat. Gods, he was slow-witted when she was near. Could he blame this on the head injury, too? "Not yet. To be honest, I don't really know what to look for. I don't even know where they found me."

Something flickered across her expression, then it was gone. Olivia pointed past him, further into the cave.

"Through there. You were lying across a crack in the floor, with the light filtering around you."

"You were there?" Jackson rasped. His heart thudded in his chest, and for the dozenth time since waking, he was struck by the uncanny sensation that his body knew something he didn't.

Olivia cocked her head. "Of course. You didn't know that?"

Of course? Jackson wet his lips. "It seems there's a lot I don't know."

She huffed a laugh, but there was no real amusement there. She sounded bitter. Tired. But she offered him a faint smile, patting his arm as she led the way. That small contact sent goosebumps rippling over his skin, and he followed her careful footsteps with a frown.

The cave was deep and maze-like, but true to Olivia's word, they didn't walk much further. Bats rustled and chattered overhead, drops of water and the gods knew what else dropping noisily onto the worn stone. And when he rounded a boulder and saw the golden wash of light, he knew this was where he'd been.

Not just from the stories. From everyone else's accounts of the cave.

Recognition tugged at Jackson's gut. He'd been here before.

The light was warm and bright, dust motes spinning in its rays, but he kept a careful distance. Just because something looked friendly did not mean it couldn't do harm.

Just look at this librarian, for example. She was small and pale; she wore simple clothes and thick-framed glasses, yet her disapproval when aimed at him sliced clean though his chest.

"It's safe," she murmured, like she could hear his thoughts.

"As far as we can tell, the light is what kept you alive."

"Not *here*, though. Right?" He watched her closely as she approached the crack in the stone, dropping clumsily to her knees. Her ankle still hurt, then. "My body stayed in this cave for all those months, but I was out there. With you."

She glanced over her shoulder, her smile forced. "Yes, that's right."

There were so many questions. So many things he needed to know. Like: did he bother her? Was she glad to be rid of him? What did they do together, all that time? Were they friends, or was he like a creepy stalker, haunting her every move? By the gods, were they *more*?

Did she miss him? Did she feel the same pull that he did, a fishhook caught in his chest?

He didn't ask. Maybe he could have at one point—the first time she visited him in hospital, perhaps. But he'd squandered that chance, too eager to be alone with his thoughts, and now she was closed off to him. Wary and cold.

Olivia sat back on her heels, staring down into the crack. The flickering light danced in her icy blonde hair and painted her skin the color of cream. Jackson watched her, lost in the sight, and almost forgot to look around the cave until a leopard prowled through a gap in the rock. He spun around, cheeks burning, pretending to study the ancient paintings on the cave walls.

When Danny returned a minute later, human and dressed, his expression was half amused, half exasperated.

"Anything?" he urged. Jackson shrugged helplessly.

"Olivia knows more than I do. Sorry, man."

"Liv?"

"I'm sorry, Danny."

The shifter's shoulders slumped. He raked a hand through his tawny hair.

"There's something here. He was knocked out cold! There's no way Jackson's body got out of the river on its own. Plus, there are scent trails all through the cave, and that sound..." Danny trailed off, frowning at the cave paintings on the far wall. "Give me a minute, you two."

Jackson shoved his hands in his pockets, gazing up at the writhing carpet of bats on the cave roof. Danny picked over the cave paintings, and Olivia stretched her ankle in slow circles, and Jackson tried not to fixate on the police officer's careless words.

You two.

You two.

It meant nothing. And he was suffering from a head injury. That was all.

* * *

The police station's evidence locker reminded Jackson of his sponsors' warehouses. With each expedition, they'd call him in and announce proudly—for the cameras—that he could have any piece of gear his heart desired. Top of the range drones and body cameras to document his efforts; military-grade survival kit. He'd wheeled a cart around those warehouses like a kid in a candy store, picking out the objects that would keep him company over the coming weeks or months.

Those warehouses were packed but orderly. They smelled like packing foam and unbroken leather.

The evidence locker, on the other hand, smelled like the bottom of the mystery bin at a thrift store. Wire cages lined one wall, holding back an avalanche of lost property—threadbare backpacks; the tangled sleeves of sweaters; dusty cameras on frayed neck straps. Shelves lined another, holding cardboard boxes labelled in a messy scrawl. And steel cabinets took up the remaining space, locking away whatever illegal contraband was seized in a town like Boiling River.

"Drugs," Danny said, answering Jackson's unasked question. "Some small weaponry. Unregistered magical objects."

Jackson cleared his throat and nodded, turning to the wire cages. His rescued gear was wedged somewhere in there.

The single bulb hanging from the ceiling didn't cast light so much as create shadows. The evening sky was inky black through the small window set high up on the wall like a prison cell.

"Any ideas where to start?" Jackson eyed the cages doubtfully. The items inside were bursting through the mesh, promising to fall in a landslide the second he opened one.

Danny shrugged cheerfully. "Nope. Keep an eye out for mice, though. There's a nest of them somewhere in there. And just in case you get any ideas," the shifter pointed at the red light of a camera, "remember you're being watched."

The door swung shut behind the officer as he strolled down the corridor whistling. The man's moods were a mess—that morning, he'd been almost scarily intense, grinding his teeth over the unanswered riddles of the cave. And now, after a full shift in this precinct, he'd met Jackson in the lobby with an upbeat grin.

"Alright," Jackson muttered, running a hand through his hair. "Time to get to work."

He fell into a steady rhythm, working to the pulse of the radio speakers clustered on one wall. Their sound was tinny

103

and crackled with static, but the beat of each song seemed to sync up with his heart pumping in his chest. Jackson sang under his breath as he worked, sorting through the landslide of junk on the ground, a mouse skittering over one shoe. He didn't even hear the door open behind him until a voice cut through his off-key chorus.

"Cas-Jackson. Um, hi. Danny said you were in here."

He whirled around, a discarded umbrella in one hand. "Olivia!" He tossed the umbrella onto the pile. "Yeah. Uh. What's up?"

Heat crept up his neck. *What's up?* Gods, he was like a teenager around her.

Olivia stepped further into the room, eyeing the piles of junk at his feet.

"What are you looking for?"

"Huh? Oh. My gear."

She frowned slightly, nudging an old coat with her toe. "Won't your sponsors give you new stuff?"

"Yeah, but they're not here. If I want to try the river again, I'll need to use the same kit."

"Try it again. Try the river again." Her voice was flat. "You can't be serious."

Irritation swept through him, stiffening his limbs. Jackson folded his arms and glared at the prim librarian. She still wore the shorts and t-shirt from earlier, though now she had a green chunky knit cardigan piled around her shoulders. It swamped her, dangling past her shorts to mid-thigh, and shit, that should not turn him on so much.

Not when she was being an ass. Sticking her pert little nose into his business.

"This is my job," he snapped, turning away from her to

keep sorting. He didn't want to see that disappointed frown anymore. "Was there something you wanted?" His voice was curt, layered with dismissal, and a pang of regret shot through him when he heard her sharp intake of breath.

"No," Olivia choked. "Not from you."

"Then get out!" Jackson wheeled around, jabbing a finger at the door. He didn't even know himself right now, but something about her words had sliced clean through to his core. His pulse pounded in his ears, his breath sawing raggedly through his lungs, and when she flinched back, he could have howled at the ceiling.

The door slammed shut behind her, the flap of her cardigan whipping through the gap. Jackson stood alone, his ears ringing. That was... bad. He needed to go after her and apologize. She'd done so much for him and this is how he repaid her? He stumbled toward the exit, a thermos flying off his boot, but as he reached for the door handle, his body froze.

That was... him. His voice. Echoing from the radio. A cheesy jingle played from the speakers, advertising the local palm reader, but the commercial was drowned out by his urgent, panicked tones. He called out, voice hoarse and desperate, explaining that he'd lost his body and needed help—

Jackson staggered back and leaned on a table, the metal legs creaking under his weight. His heart pounded so fast in his chest, he could barely breathe. Sweat prickled over his skin, a bead sliding down his spine, and his hand shook as he scrubbed at his face.

That voice—that was him—

Memories bombarded him, slamming into him one after the other.

Waking up in the town square.

Exploding into atoms in the desert.

Screaming until his throat tore for someone to hear him.

Reaching into Olivia's bathtub—

Olivia.

Caspian buried his face in his hands. She'd come looking for him, so tentative and shy, and he'd yelled at her to leave. She worried for him, didn't want him to risk his freaking life a second time, and he'd *yelled*.

Bile rose in his throat.

Caspian scrambled for the wastepaper bin, a thousand memories clamoring in his ears, and threw up his lunch.

Chapter Thirteen

When Olivia was upset, she went to the library. It was a source of constant exasperation for Bree.

"You work here," she'd plead, tugging at Olivia's sleeve. *"By the gods, don't come here for free."*

Olivia didn't care. When you'd wrestled with insomnia for half your life, you couldn't afford to be picky. This helped, so this was where she came. Shelving books until the witching hour passed.

A single lamp lit the library, pooling golden light around a distant armchair. This was one of Olivia's first changes when she'd taken the job: reading nooks and hidden spaces. Libraries were for tucking yourself away and escaping to other worlds.

And for running from your problems, apparently.

Jackson's words from the evidence locker echoed around his skull. The way he'd pointed at the door, telling her to leave; the angry flush to his cheeks.

He was right, of course. An ass, but a correct one.

It was none of her business.

She had no right to swan in there and tell him what to do. To judge him for picking up where he left off, for getting back to his real life. The one without her.

Olivia hefted a hardback tome in her hand, scanning the title. It was a kid's reference book on the local dinosaur digs—one of her favorites. She crouched and slid it onto the shelf.

She didn't stand up for a long time, crouching there on the tiles, counting her breaths in and out.

Breathe.

Breathe.

She could handle this. She could handle anything.

A pang of homesickness rippled through her gut, and Olivia clutched at the nearest shelf until her knuckles turned white. She still hadn't visited her mother. She'd been so wrapped up in Caspian, then hanging around Jackson like a kicked puppy.

Tomorrow. She'd go tomorrow.

And she'd stay out of Jackson's way until he was safely out of town.

The library door creaked open, far away behind the stacks. Olivia sighed and pushed to her feet.

"I'll be there in a minute!"

She'd spent so many nights in this library, word had gotten around the supernatural community that the library was open sometimes at night. When she came here to clear her thoughts, more often than not she found herself checking out books for the local vampires.

She scrubbed her sleeve over her face. Her face was blotchy and drawn in the reflection on the dark windows, but the vampires were used to it. They probably thought this was her normal face.

"Olivia," a voice said at the end of the stack. Her eyes slammed shut. No, this wasn't happening.

"We're closed, actually," she ground out, her throat tight. Maybe it was rude, but she couldn't see him. Couldn't deal with him right now.

Not here. Not in the one place she came to escape.

"I'll go," he promised quickly. "I just came to apologize." He swallowed audibly. "I'm so sorry. I can't believe I spoke to you like that."

Olivia risked a glance. Jackson stood at the end of the stacks, his arms dangling at his sides. His chest heaved beneath his white t-shirt, and he stared at her, anguished and intense.

Ooh-kay. She forced a smile. "It's fine. You're right. It's none of my business."

"It is your business." He stepped closer, the shadows shifting across his face. "I'm your business. If you want me to be."

It wasn't fair. Gods, it wasn't fair.

"Caspian was my business." She clenched her sleeves in her damp palms. "But you... I don't know you. Good luck, though." She waved vaguely at the window. "With the river. And everything else."

She was wishing him luck, letting him off the hook. So why did he look so freaking unhappy? His shoulders slumped as she spoke, and his throat bobbed as he swallowed.

"What if I don't go?" he croaked. "I could stay here. With you."

Her heart slammed against her rib cage. This was what she'd wanted, what she'd pined for so badly. But this wasn't her Caspian—he was a stranger wearing her lover's face. Bitterness churned in her gut.

"I don't want you," she hissed. "I wanted Caspian. And now he's gone and you're here instead." She raked her gaze over him, from the top of his head to his feet. "It's like a bad joke."

"Don't say that."

"Why not?" She shoved at her cart, pushing it down the aisle toward him. He scrambled out of her way, pressing up against the shelves. "We're finally being honest with each other. It's healthy, don't you think?"

He caught her elbow as she stormed past, his warm hand gripping her in the same spot Caspian had steadied her so many times. Olivia's breath caught in her throat, her chest throbbing, and she turned in his hold. They slammed back against the shelves, pressing into the kiss, mouths biting and hands tearing, sealing together so tightly that they should have morphed into one.

"This means nothing," she growled into his mouth. Damn, who even was she? "This is closure. That's all."

He grunted as she dropped to her knees, yanking his top button open. Olivia paused, breathing in hard through her nose. She glared up at him, eyes glinting.

"Yes?"

He gripped the shelves so hard, the wood creaked.

"I've started to remember," he told her, breaking off as she pressed her forehead to his hip, screwing her eyes shut.

"Yes or no, Jackson?"

"Call me Caspian," he pleaded.

"No." She sat back on her heels. "You're not him." She pulled her hands back, getting ready to stand, but he grabbed her wrists in a loose hold.

"Wait. Yes, I want this. Please don't stop."

She grumbled under her breath, but knelt forward again. Her fingers shook as she tugged down his zipper.

"I'll prove it to you, sweetheart," he murmured above her,

his fingers playing in her hair. "I've remembered. Things are different now." She swallowed him down just to shut him up.

It was ironic, really. She and Caspian could never have done this. He flickered out of being too easily, especially when he lost focus, which happened a lot when her hands were on him. And now, with Jackson, her hands were everywhere, stroking and kneading and raking her fingernails down the front of his thighs. She bobbed her head steadily, working her tongue over him, and the anxieties that gnawed at her about her inexperience faded away as he let out a broken groan.

"You made me come once," she told him raggedly, pulling off him with a pop. "Do you remember that?"

"Yes," he hissed, surprising her. If he truly remembered the night in her bathroom, then maybe—

No. She slammed that thought out. She wouldn't get her hopes up again. She couldn't—this was where she wound up, sad and aimless, shelving books about dinosaurs after midnight. Olivia leaned forward, taking him back in her mouth before she could say something she might regret.

"Sweetheart," Jackson groaned out. She screwed her eyes shut. Caspian called her that. "Sweetheart, I'm going to—"

She pressed closer, relishing the shudder of his muscled thighs as he fell apart. His hands were buried in her hair, scratching at her skull, and she could have purred if she wasn't so hollow.

When she sat back on her heels, wiping her sleeve over her mouth, satisfaction coursed through her at the sight of him. The cocky explorer—the man who'd told her to leave—he was ruined. Disheveled and breathless.

"Time to go." She pushed to her feet. "I'm going too," she added, to soften the blow. She wasn't kicking him out; she wanted to be alone. Curled up in her big empty bed with her arms wrapped around herself.

"Okay." Jackson's voice was gravelly. Like he'd been the one on his knees. "Okay. Can I see you tomorrow?"

Tell him no, a voice in her head screamed, even as she shrugged.

"It's a small town. I might see you around."

For the first time since he stepped into the dark library, a grin tugged his mouth. This man really did love a challenge.

"Tomorrow, then. Goodnight, sweetheart."

"Goodnight," she whispered. When his footsteps echoed out of the library, she sagged back against the shelves.

What the hell had come over her?

And what was she thinking, agreeing to see him again?

* * *

There were many things to love about Bree Mendez, but for Olivia, one of them was her friend's night owl status. On the worst nights, when sleep was unthinkable, Bree was inevitably awake, too.

Sure, she caught up in the daytime, slobbing around her apartment above the Silver Bullet in her pajamas. But company was company, and even if Bree didn't know firsthand how insomnia felt, she always swept Olivia up in her arms and squeezed.

"Sit." Bree ordered now, waving at a bar stool. The Silver Bullet was closing up, the staff wiping down the tables, but Bree swiped a clean glass and a bottle of gin off the shelf. She poured a generous measure into the glass, hunting down some juice for mixer while Olivia watched, her chin in her hand.

"What would I do without you?"

Bree snorted. "Learn to love Hex Mex."

Olivia wrinkled her nose. Boiling River's biggest nightclub was rowdy and wicked. It was a dark, devious place with pounding music and writhing bodies.

Bree loved it. And whenever she was there, Olivia spent the whole night fantasizing about reading and eating ice cream in her pajamas.

"Want to talk about it?" Bree watched her out of the corner of her eye. Olivia shrugged.

"There's not much to say."

"I doubt that, somehow." Bree's frown softened as Otis Pascale, the town's alpha werewolf and her fated mate, burst through the bar doorway. He strode across the floorboards, boots echoing, and rounded the bar with a sly grin.

"Girls' night, huh?" He pressed a kiss to Bree's neck, wrapping her in his arms. The sight made Olivia's heart throb. "Must have lost my invite."

"You don't qualify," Bree said, voice dry. But a faint smile curled her lips, and she turned in his arms to kiss him hello.

The gin burned the back of Olivia's throat. Who needed mixer? She poured herself another inch.

"I blew Jackson," she said conversationally when they turned back around. Otis spluttered a laugh, and Bree elbowed him in the ribs. "So you can add that to my list of bad decisions."

"Why?" Otis asked. "Was he into something freaky?"

Olivia tossed back another drink.

"No," she ground out, slamming the glass on the bar. "He was normal, and a gentleman, and he called me sweetheart."

"That bastard." Otis' eyes twinkled. "I'll tear him limb from limb."

She dropped her forehead onto the bar. It was no use. There was only gin, and the hope that maybe Jackson would suffer another convenient head wound by the morning.

Nothing lethal. Just enough for him to forget what she'd done.

Maybe she could use one, too.

Chapter Fourteen

Caspian waited outside Olivia's building with two croissants and a plan. The dawn painted the Boiling River streets rose gold, and the more industrious of the local pigeons pecked at the sidewalk. The pastries were warm inside their paper bag, cradled gently in his palm.

Olivia was a lady. A romantic. She sighed over Austen heroes and pressed dried flowers between the pages of her books.

No problem. That worked for him. He might never have tried to be romantic before, but then he'd never dated Olivia. Turned out, when he had a chance with the world's most gorgeous woman, he wanted to be her Mr Darcy.

And he had to believe he had a chance. Otherwise, what was the point of all this? The trauma and the heartache; his life turned upside down.

It was all worth it, if she'd give him a smile.

"Morning," he called as she walked down her building's steps, eyes widening in surprise when she saw him. She looked tired, dark shadows clinging beneath her eyes, but beautiful nonetheless. He held up the paper bag. "I know it's not the same as striding toward you across a moor, but we have to work with the surroundings."

Her mouth twitched. Triumph roared through his chest.

Watching her peel open the bag and inhale the steam rising out of it made his pulse settle for the first time in days. He'd bring her a thousand croissants. He'd sell his life's possessions to buy pastries. He'd—

"About last night." She cringed. "I hope I didn't, um. Scare you?"

He shook his head so hard his ears rang.

"Of course not. I loved it. I mean, I'd obviously like it better if you were happy—"

"That's okay, then." She cut him off gently, plucking a croissant out of the bag. She smiled at him shyly before taking a bite, flecks of pastry drifting onto her top.

Caspian balled his hands into fists, shoving them into his jeans to keep from reaching for her. He wanted to brush those crumbs off, but he had no right touching her there, and besides—once he started, he'd never stop.

"What are you doing today?"

"Work," she mumbled around a bite. Obviously. He could have kicked himself. Something about her made him sixteen again, gawky and flushed.

"I was thinking I could come?" She hesitated. He rushed on. "I mean, I've spent the day with you there loads of times before, right?"

She nodded, eyes suddenly sad.

No. No, no. That wasn't the plan. The plan was to shower her with gifts and bring her endless food; to leave her sweet notes and take her out on dates. All the things she sighed over in her books. His plan did not include her eyes brimming with tears.

"I don't have to," he said quickly. "It was just an idea."

She chewed on her lip. "Maybe you could come and visit? For a little while."

"Great," he blurted, before she could change her mind. "Perfect. I will do that."

This was fine. Better, even. This way he could spend the morning finding her a gift in the Boiling River shops. Something that said, *I'm still the ghost you remember, but solid now!*

Something like that.

He watched her walk down the street, the sunlight glinting in her hair, and steeled himself.

He would make this work.

* * *

Caspian had never really watched Rom Coms. On the rare occasions he watched a movie in his old life, it had been a horror movie, or a documentary. Sometimes a mindless thriller.

He wished he'd watched more, now. Trying to win Olivia over was like taking a pop quiz without having studied. He peered at a shelf of trinkets in the town emporium—a bright and bizarre shop which displayed ancient magical objects and embroidered Boiling River aprons with equal enthusiasm. There were crystals and tiny cacti; ceramic figurines and glowing buttons.

Nothing that said, *Please spend your life with me! I'm dying here!*

"Can I help you, dearie?"

A tiny round woman peered up at him beneath a tuft of white hair. Hundreds of wrinkles shifted on her face as she spoke, and when she grinned, there was orange lipstick on her teeth.

"Uh." Caspian scratched the back of his head. "I'm looking for a gift."

"Oooh," the woman crooned, her beaded shawls rustling as she inched closer. "A gift for a girlfriend?"

He swallowed hard. What the hell? He could endure some humiliation if it helped with his plan.

"Yes. Well. I hope so."

The woman's gnarled hands clapped together, their long, sharp fingernails painted purple.

"Oh, dearie. I know just what you need."

Her name was Mabel, he learned, as they combed the shelves together. She stuck to his side, her perfume tickling his nose as she jabbed him in the gut.

"What does she like, your girl?"

"Books. Cooking. Vintage clothes and pretty things."

Mabel hummed, prodding a snow globe. The finger inside staggered against the glass, flipping her off. "Yes, wonderful."

The other shoppers were deemed unimportant, left to line up by the cash register unheeded until they lost patience and stormed out. Mabel ignored them all, even their angry calls, clucking over bouquets of dried wildflowers and necklaces made from animal bones. Caspian surveyed the items too, doubt curling in his stomach. Would Olivia even like any of this?

At one point, Mabel stifled a burp, then turned to the side and screamed. It was a banshee scream, unmistakable in its horror, freezing his blood in his veins. The sound was an assault on his ears, slicing through his eardrums, then it was gone as quickly as it started.

"Excuse me, precious," Mabel murmured, peering inside a jar of dragon scales. "I get terrible indigestion."

"I don't..." Caspian trailed off, then tried again. "This stuff isn't right. It's not her."

Mabel clucked, plucking his hand from his pocket and turning it over in her grip. She smoothed a gnarled thumb over his palm, muttering to herself, then brought it up to her nose and sniffed.

"Uh." He stood there dumbly as she sniffed at his palm, then moved her nose along his wrist. His hand was almost comically large in hers, bigger than her face, but she ignored him, the cold tip of her nose dragging along his skin.

"I've got it." She dropped his hand like a rock. It smacked against his thigh. "Follow me." She led him deeper into the emporium, through winding aisles and shifting puddles of light. They passed walls of curled carpets, their fringes twitching; they stepped over cardboard boxes filled with enchanted gold.

"Don't take any of that," Mabel threw over her shoulder. "Not even to buy. It's not for good boys like you."

Caspian felt more like an old man than a boy, but he said nothing, striding around the boxes untempted. When they reached a bare wall at the end of an aisle, he blinked around at the shelves.

They were dusty. Cluttered with nonsense trinkets. Useless.

"I'm not sure—" he began, but Mabel rummaged inside her ample cleavage and pulled out a large brass key. She fed it into a crack in the wall, turning it smoothly to the side.

Thunk. The wall swung open.

"Only my favorites come back here," she told him, batting her eyelids over her shoulder. "These treasures aren't for everyone, oh dear, no."

Caspian followed her into the darkness.

* * *

He left the parcel on Olivia's desk. She was busy anyway, reading to the local children. They sat wide-eyed and open-mouthed—a fair representation of how he felt around her—listening in rapt quiet as she read them tales of knights and dragons.

When she read the battle scenes, they gasped and clutched their feet. When she did funny voices, they laughed.

It was ridiculously charming. Caspian leaned against a distant bookshelf, watching with a smile on his face.

No wonder he'd haunted her of all people. How could he possibly choose any different? She was a marvel. He'd been an idiot not to see it the second he woke up, but he'd been dazed, battered and bewildered.

He could kick himself now. She'd been right there, bringing him flowers and grapes and fussing over his hospital bed.

"Good, isn't she?" The voice made him jump. A redhead stood at his shoulder.

Claire, he remembered. He cleared his throat, nodding.

"Hi. You drew my pentagram."

Claire beamed, shaking his offered hand.

"I did! We should do it again sometime."

Caspian winced, remembering the pain ripping through his muscles, straining his tendons where they latched to his bones.

"Maybe," he hedged. He turned back to Olivia. "She's perfect," he said, answering her earlier question. Claire hummed happily, fiddling with the strap of her painter's overalls. She was an odd match for that glowering, well-groomed vampire.

"Olivia is stubborn." The statement came unprompted. Caspian turned to her, eyebrows raised. "Everyone thinks she's all quiet and shy, but when she sets her mind it's very hard to change it."

"Are you telling me to stop trying?" he asked, stomach sinking.

"No." Claire smirked. "I'm telling you to buckle in. It'll be a rough ride."

"She's worth it." Caspian turned back to the reading session, his heart calming again. Even if the artist had tried to warn him away, he wouldn't have listened.

Olivia's blonde hair cascaded over one shoulder, tickling at the pages of the picture book propped up in her lap.

He chewed the inside of his cheek.

He was jealous. Of a book.

"All that time, I couldn't touch her. Not properly." He scrubbed a hand down his face. "Now here I am, back at square one."

"Not quite square one." Claire cocked her head, grinning. "From what I hear, she already put you through your paces."

Caspian spluttered. "That's not—she told you?" Hope soared in his chest. She couldn't regret it that much if she'd told her friends. And she couldn't have been as unaffected as she seemed, if she rushed off to confide in someone.

He stifled a grin, rolling his eyes at the redhead's smirk.

It would be childish to ask what she'd said. To ask for Olivia's account, word-for-word. He clamped his mouth shut and watched her read.

He didn't mind that she'd told her friends. Whatever dignity he had left, she could have it. As long as it was his name in her mouth, and him on her mind.

Chapter Fifteen

" I set up cameras." Danny threw himself into the spare chair by her desk. Olivia raised her eyebrows, leaning back in her seat. The library was quiet, the stacks empty except for one chubby fly, buzzing as it threw itself against a windowpane.

Boiling River was not an after-lunch town. The sun was too hot, and the people too sleepy from eating.

Boiling River was not a morning town either, for that matter. Nor were the residents fans of late afternoon. They collectively came alive at night when the sky darkened and the air cooled. Then, the locals spilled out of their homes, restless and rowdy as they strode over the still-baking sidewalks.

"Cameras? Where?"

"By the river."

Olivia blew out a breath. "Should you be telling me this?"

Danny shrugged. "They closed the investigation. So now I'm looking into it in my free time. As a private citizen."

"A private citizen with access to police recording equipment."

Danny winked. "Exactly."

She shouldn't encourage this. As a friend, she should talk him down, persuade him to move on. But Olivia was curious, too. Maybe it didn't eat her up from the inside like it did with Danny, but it was an unsolved puzzle. She liked puzzles.

Plus, it was about Caspian. As much as she hated to admit it, he was still her favorite subject.

"Have you got anything yet?"

Danny twitched his head to the side, annoyed. "Shadows. Shapes. There's something in the water. But I don't know yet if it's related to the cave."

"Did you set cameras there too?"

"Of course." Danny rolled his brown eyes. "I'm not a complete moron, Liv." He sat forward, the chair creaking beneath his weight. Danny was a big man—slim but tall and corded with muscle. His white button-down shirt strained across his chest.

If they hadn't grown up friends, if she wasn't weirdly obsessed with an ex-ghost, she might ogle him. Harbor a crush on Danny instead of the explorer with a death wish. She tried now, squinting at the shape of Danny's muscles beneath his shirt.

"Liv?" He glanced down at himself, brushing off invisible crumbs. "What's wrong? You look like you've been sucking on a lemon."

"Just tired," she mumbled. Shit. It was useless.

She was doomed the moment she saw his gift, placed carefully on her desk. He'd lined it up so the edge of the package was perfectly parallel to the edge of the wood. That alone had made her chest throb.

And when she opened it? Forget it. That hardback book called to her soul. It whispered to her as she traced her fingertips over the worn leather.

A first edition. Moby Dick. With paper so thin, it crackled as she turned the pages. The scent of sea water clung to the book, and the cry of the seagulls she'd never heard echoed in her mind. And those hand-drawn illustrations, scored in black ink, every pen stroke still so clear…

Olivia fanned herself, giving Danny a quick smile.

"Tell me if you find something."

He nodded, pushing to his feet. "I will." He turned back as he paused in the library doorway. "Oh, and tell your boy I've found his gear. He can take on the river again as soon as he likes."

She agreed somehow, her voice faint. The way Danny said that was like it was a *good* thing. That it was admirable to set yourself against a mystical river until it killed you once and for all.

Men. Olivia tossed her glasses onto the desk with a clatter, rubbing at her eyes.

There was not enough gin in the world.

* * *

"Hey, stranger."

She didn't even have to look for Jackson. She'd been fully prepared to stomp through the town, propelled by righteous ire. But here he was, waiting in the Boiling River town square, his hands in his jeans pockets and a soft smile on his face.

Her pulse skipped. No. She would not do this again. Never mind the book he gave her.

"Danny was here," she called, a hard edge to her voice. Was she imagining things, or did a muscle pop in his jaw?

"Oh?" He watched her intently, stepping closer across the paving stones. "What did he want?"

Olivia rolled her eyes. She'd dropped to her knees for this man, and yet here he was growling like a jealous caveman.

"He says he found your gear. You can go risk your life again." She smiled tightly. "Congratulations."

She barged past him, dodging a man packing away a table of treasure maps for sale as the evening light drained away. But she'd barely walked three steps before Jackson was at her side keeping pace.

"I'm not going back on the river."

She couldn't look at him. "No?"

"No. I told you, I remembered everything. Why the hell would I go back out there?"

Olivia snorted, lengthening her stride. A ruffled pigeon hopped out of her way. "Why would you anyway? It was an idiot move before."

"But now I have you." He caught her elbow, pulling her to a stop. People flowed around them, grumbling. Jackson scrubbed the back of his head. "I had you, anyway. And I haven't given up." He tilted her chin up, forcing her to drag her eyes off the ground. "Why would I risk everything when I finally have something to hope for?"

Her heart drummed in her chest. "You didn't before?"

"Not like this." He stepped closer until their chests were brushing.

"Jackson," Olivia whispered. His eyes fell shut, his expression pained.

"Please. Call me Caspian."

She wet her lips. If she did this, if she accepted it was really him, that meant... that meant...

126

Her future rose up before her, glorious and terrifying. Olivia squared her shoulders. She cleared her throat. She didn't run away from anything.

"Caspian." She said it forcefully. Loud and sure. And it was worth it for the relief and gratitude which broke over his face, his scars shifting as he beamed down at her.

"You won't regret this."

She smirked. "See that I don't."

He grabbed her hand and started pulling. Down the street—down toward her apartment where they would be finally, solidly alone. She tripped after him, something swelling in her chest, before something poked at her memory.

"Wait." Olivia tugged him to a stop. "I have somewhere I need to go."

"Now?" He looked so tragic, she burst out laughing. He grinned back, rueful.

"Yes," she told him. "Now. But... you could come. If you like."

"Where are we going?" he asked immediately, already tucking his hand in hers. Olivia chewed on her lip, doubt already gnawing at her insides. If she showed him this, he might change his mind. It might be too real suddenly, too scary.

Faith. She would have faith. Like the heroines in her books. Olivia squeezed his hand, her palm clammy.

"To see the ghost of Christmas future."

* * *

When her mother first got ill, Olivia had been a teenager. By turns shy and sullen, chaotic hormones coursing through her veins, she'd been a handful. She felt so guilty about that later.

It started with mood swings. Usually so steady, Olivia's

mother began to match her daughter for outbursts with manic highs and crashing lows. Then there were patches in her memory—conversations forgotten, keys misplaced.

Then the voices began.

Olivia preferred not to dwell on that time. On those horrible months before her mom got treatment. Even now, panic made her heart pound and palms sweat when she went to visit.

But at least here, her mom was stable. Content.

The home was isolated in the desert, part way between Boiling River and the next town. They drove there mostly in silence, Olivia clutching the steering wheel as Caspian rubbed soothing circles on her knee with his thumb.

"Coyote." Olivia nodded out the window.

"Chimera," Caspian said, pointing out the other side.

They passed the drive with the hum of the radio and the soft sounds of their shared breaths. The truck tires rumbled over the pockmarked dirt, and Olivia slowed now and then to let rattle snakes slither off the road.

"When you say ghost of Christmas future…"

"My mother." She shot him a tight smile. "It was a joke. A bad one. She's… not well."

Caspian's thumb rubbed steady circles. Round, around, around, his calloused thumb smoothing over her vintage tea dress.

The truck swayed over a rough patch in the road, before turning onto the home's dirt driveway. This place was a mirror of the fancy mansions she always saw in movies, but instead of palm trees and fountains lining the path, there were twenty-foot cactus plants. They stood sentry, arms reaching towards the blushing sunset sky, their shadows shifting eerily on the ground.

Caspian said nothing as they slammed their truck doors. As they held hands and walked up to the front steps. He kept quiet even as a squat woman in a nurse's uniform answered the door, sweeping Olivia into a hug before she could say hello.

"It's been too long," the nurse said.

"I know." Olivia swallowed down her shame and jerked her head at Caspian. "But I brought entertainment."

The nurse clucked, eyes raking shamelessly down Caspian from head to toe.

"Hmm. Oh yes you did."

The visit was short but sweet. Her mother couldn't handle much more. She was curled up with a book, a frown creasing her pale forehead. But when she saw Olivia, she jumped to her feet, tugging her in for a bony hug.

She should have come sooner. Gods, that was shameful. She'd never leave it so long again.

"Mom." Olivia yanked Caspian to her side, taking his hand and squeezing. "This is Caspian. My, um. My…"

"Boyfriend?" he offered, lips curling. She loosed a breath.

"Yeah. That works. Boyfriend."

"How wonderful to meet you," her mother breathed, widening her eyes at Olivia meaningfully. She shrugged. Yeah, even beaten up by the river, he was gorgeous.

"That explains it," Caspian mused later as they strolled back to the truck. The stars were brighter, the darkness deeper, and ribbons of magic twirled and twisted over the mountains. "Why you didn't think I was real for so long."

Olivia shrugged, uncomfortable. "Yeah, I thought I was losing it." She laughed, but it was too brassy, too loud. "It might be hereditary. Who knows?" She risked a glance, but it was too dark to make out his expression. "Would that change things?"

He tightened his grip on her hand. "No. Never."

It was easy, after that, to nudge him back to her truck. To whisper promises in his ear of what awaited them at home. *Their* home, if he wanted it to be. And judging by his moan as she nipped his throat, he did.

Chapter Sixteen

*I*f Caspian didn't get his hands on Olivia in the next ten minutes, he was going to explode into atoms just like he used to. But this time, he wouldn't reform in the town square. No; he'd be a fine red mist on the Boiling River streets—a monument to sexual frustration.

"Come on," he tugged her down the sidewalk. "Have mercy. Walk faster."

"This is fast. We don't all have two-meter long legs."

"Don't make me throw you over my shoulder."

"Don't make me bite your ass from up there."

Gods. Should he like that idea? Probably not.

Caspian didn't care.

"Right, you asked for it." He turned to her, arms outstretched, but the grin slid off his face as he saw the leopard loping toward them. It streaked over paving stones, muscles bunching under its fur, its every movement a testament to lithe grace.

"Gods damn it." Caspian pinched the bridge of his nose as the leopard shot into the nearest alley, Olivia spinning to watch it go. A few moments later, Danny emerged, bare chested and naked except for a worn pair of jeans.

"Do you just keep those lying around town?" Caspian snapped.

Danny gave him a weird look. "Yeah. Of course. All the shifters do." The jeans were slung low on his hips as he crossed to Olivia.

Perfect.

"I found it, Liv." His eyes were bright, his chest heaving.

She frowned. "You figured it out?"

"Yep." He popped the p. Caspian fought not to roll his eyes, reminding himself sternly that he liked this man, and Danny had done nothing but help him.

But did he have to wander around without a shirt? Caspian rubbed at the scars on his cheek, suddenly self-conscious.

"Come to the river. I'll show you."

No, Caspian howled internally.

"Sure," Olivia said.

This was karma. He'd wronged a deity. He was cursed. It was *something*.

Danny turned to him next. "You coming, man?"

"Yes," he ground out. Wherever Olivia went, he'd follow. And besides, the river was dangerous—as he'd demonstrated so well himself.

They walked across the desert, because of course they did. Why drive, or make this night go any faster, when you could go for a leisurely stroll? Caspian rubbed at his eyes.

As they wove through the scattered boulders and clumps of cacti, bright blue bursts of fire shot out of the ground on both sides. They were desert spirits, or lost souls returning from below. There were a lot of theories and folk tales.

132

Either way, he inched closer to Olivia's side. He may not be supernatural, but he'd take on a freaky blue spirit if needed.

"I kept seeing those shadows on the footage. First in the water, then something slipping into the cave. So I tried different angles, and flew a drone over, and lowered a heat resistant camera into the water..." Danny chattered about his methods as they walk, the happiest Caspian had ever seen him since solving his puzzle. He was still shirtless, his tawny hair tugged by the breeze, but Olivia didn't seem distracted. If anything, she toyed with Caspian's fingers more and more as they walked.

"Where's this going, Danny?" Olivia interrupted. He beamed at her.

"There's an unregistered supernatural in Boiling River."

Caspian snorted. "And that makes you happy? I thought you were a cop?"

Danny tapped his nose, eyes twinkling. "You'll see why." There was a bounce in his step as he led them along the riverbank, down the winding path to the cave. Evidence of his obsession was everywhere: the red lights of cameras winked at them, wedged between rocks, and the cable for a hydrophone trailed into the water.

"I haven't caught her yet." Danny stepped over a tripwire into the cave. "She's avoided all contact. But now that I know she's here, it's only a matter of time."

He came to a halt in the center of the cave, spreading his arms in the flickering gold light. Ancient paintings covered the walls on all sides; the bats chattered loudly overhead. Danny grinned, the sharp points of his teeth glinting in the low light.

"What's the last creature you'd expect to find in the desert?"

"A polar bear," Caspian said flatly. Olivia elbowed him in the gut.

"I don't know," she murmured. "Tell us."

Danny spun on his heel, striding to a camera wedged into a rock pile, then waved them over as he prodded the screen.

"Look." He shoved it under their noses. Caspian squinted in the gloom. The screen was dark too, a patchwork of shadows, and he could just make out a shape walking past the lens and out of the cave where it slid into the water.

Caspian glanced at Olivia. She shrugged back. Danny tipped back his head and growled.

"Look again." He zoomed in this time, jabbing a finger at the shape. It looked... feminine. Like a human woman. But as it slid into the water...

"Huh." Caspian leaned closer, frowning.

"A mermaid," Danny breathed, snatching the camera away and staring down at the screen, utterly absorbed. When he glanced up at them, something danced in his eyes. "There's a mermaid in the desert."

* * *

They burst into the apartment, the door banging off the wall. Olivia's cardigan hung off one shoulder, her hair mussed up and wild from the trip up the stairs. Caspian sucked in a shaky breath, spinning her around and pressing her into the wall. She arched up against him, her soft curves to his hard chest, and his forehead dropped onto her shoulder. He ground his hips against her as he spoke, barely able to form the words.

"Sweetheart. If Danny walks in before I get my hands on you—"

"Likewise." She tugged at his t-shirt, stretching the fabric. "Off. Off."

"Yes, ma'am." He yanked it over his head, tossing it onto the floorboards. Then he paused as she scrabbled at his bare skin, remembering the pop of her sprained ankle. Caspian sighed, crouching to snatch up his t-shirt and lay it on the coffee table.

"Such a neat freak."

"You have slippery floorboards."

She scoffed. "Tell me about it."

It was adorable, his prim librarian accusing him of being a neat freak. She was the one obsessed with perfect right angles and parallel lines; who he'd once watched dust each pencil in her pencil pot as a ghost.

It didn't seem the right time to bring that up.

It *did* seem right to hook his forearm under her ass and boost her up until her legs wrapped around his hips. She hopped up easily, her arms winding around his neck, and gods, he'd never be able to carry a backpack again without thinking of this and flushing. He made it three steps across the living room before she sealed his mouth to his, blinding him.

Caspian groaned, kissing her back hard enough to brand her. He jiggled her higher in his arms and she whimpered, her eyes fluttering closed.

Screw it. The bedroom was a thousand miles away. They weren't going to make it.

"Forgive me," he murmured into her lips, then shoved her coffee table out the way with his boot. It rucked up the rug as it went, pulling it back from the floorboards, revealing the pentagram still chalked beneath. "Surprised you didn't clean this," he muttered as he dropped to his knees in the center. Her legs hooked tighter around his middle and she rubbed at him like a cat.

"Call it sentiment."

He spread his hand over her shoulder blades, then ran it all the way down her spine. Her back muscles twitched under his palm, and he nipped at her lip.

"I'll call it what it is. Messy."

She punched his shoulder, but a grin twisted her mouth as she fumbled with his jeans button. This wasn't what he'd pictured for their first time—he'd imagined flower petals and lit candles, the sorts of touches a girl like Olivia would want. But here she was, yanking down his zipper like a woman possessed, grinding into his lap until he saw stars.

"Are you sure?" he ground out. "We can go to the bedroom. I could put music on—"

"Caspian." She tucked her fingers into his waistband. "Do shut up."

He groaned and kissed her, losing himself in her taste, before a horrible thought tipped cold water down his back.

"I don't have a condom," he muttered, horrified at himself. Being prepared was his whole career, damn it.

She didn't even pause. Her mouth trailed along his jawline, then sucked a kiss onto his pulse point.

"I take the witches' potion. I'm not an idiot, thank you."

She was so frosty with him, even now, even as she writhed in his arms, and that drove him higher. Made him want to laugh at the ceiling. He busied himself with mapping the shape of her instead, sliding his hands inside her dress and squeezing her hips.

"This is unfair." He flicked at the collar of her dress. A line of tiny buttons ran down the center of it, each fragile-looking and fiddly. "I'm an explorer. I'm used to zips and velcro."

She snorted, leaning back on his lap to undo the first few buttons. "Never say those words to me again."

It was so easy. Yes, there were the usual awkward fumblings. They'd never done this before, and for his part at least, the pent up longing made his fingers shake. But there were no pained silences, no muttered apologies. It felt familiar somehow, as well as brand new. And when they finally got Olivia's dress off and sealed together, skin to skin, they both let out matching groans of relief.

"You're so warm," she gasped.

"You're so silky."

"That's because I'm not covered in scars and chest hair, you big brute." She smirked as she said it, running her fingertips over his muscles with unabashed greed in her eyes. He rocked against her, his pulse pounding in his ears, and reached down with trembling fingers to tug her panties to the side.

"Are you sure?" he ground out. She could roll her eyes all she wanted. He'd never stop checking.

He still had his jeans and boots on, his zipper gaping wide. But her eyes were glassy and her cheeks were flushed, just like his. She took him in hand and positioned him at her entrance.

"Yes. Are you?"

"Yes," he groaned, and she pushed him inside.

There would be other times to go slow. To explore each other's bodies; to be leisurely and decadent about it. But right now, Caspian had been coiled tight for days—for weeks, even. Months. Ever since he laid eyes on her. And apparently Olivia felt the same, since she fought to sink down on him faster; to take him deeper.

When she finally rested in his lap, fully sealed together, he dropped his forehead onto hers. Her glasses were askew, and he slid them off with careful fingers.

"Better safe than sorry," he muttered, leaning over to place them on the coffee table. She whimpered at the movement, and began to roll her hips.

He wouldn't last long. Not with her squeezing him like that, and definitely not with the love shining in her blue eyes. But her legs were already beginning to shake, letting him off the hook, and he reached down between them to rub at her core. She let out a ragged groan, her head dropping back, her hair tickling at his jean-clad thighs.

"I love you," he choked. "I've loved you for so long."

She came silently, with the tiniest squeak.

It was perfect. She was perfect, and he thrust up against her twice before following her into the abyss. And when he collapsed back against the floorboards, smearing the pentagram over the wood, she came languidly into his arms.

"I love you too," she murmured into his chest, the words muffled against his skin.

"Good." He grinned dizzily up at the ceiling. There was a hairline crack in the plaster. He'd fix that tomorrow. "That's a relief."

Epilogue

ᖰᖰᖰ

*M*usic pumped through the Boiling River town square, over the chatter of the crowds. Today was a day of bright sunshine and catchy music. Glinting trinkets tables and delicious aromas from food trucks.

The Starlight Springs witches were here, their stalls thronged with eager tourists, and Delilah and her dark-haired man stood cackling over by the booze stall. A few feet behind them, Claire painted a bright mural on the bank wall, a gang of paint-splattered teenagers helping her out.

Olivia leaned back against Caspian's chest, watching Otis and Bree compete in a limbo contest against the town kids. Otis wobbled as he crept under the pole, his teeth bared in concentration, but he hit the deck when Bree swiped his knee.

The kids burst into giggles, pointing and jumping. Bree winked at them before leaning down and whispering something in Otis' ear. He grinned and lunged up to kiss her.

Peaceful. That's how she felt, never mind the crowds and chaos. Olivia was a bookworm through and through, a creature of indoor spaces and quiet, but even she felt a blissful calm spreading through her limbs. She tipped her head back against Caspian's shoulder, closing her eyes against the baking hot desert sunshine, and soaked up the golden rays like a snake.

A flap of wings ruffled her hair. She opened one eye a crack.

A vulture perched on the bench beside Caspian, its eyes filmy and its plumage wild. A single bent feather stuck up from its head, and it lunged at Caspian snapping its beak at his shoulder.

"Alright, alright." He waved the bird away, nudging Olivia to sit up. "I'll be right back, sweetheart. You want a taco?"

She shook her head, blinking at the bird as he plunged into the crowd.

It was huge up close. Bigger than she'd guessed when she passed the vultures before in the town square. It settled down on its perch, its talons scratching at the wood, and cocked its head at her as if to say… *"And what?"*

She blew out a breath, turning back to the limbo. Outdoorsy people made the weirdest friends. At least when Caspian went on trips these days, he didn't tend to bring them home.

Except for that one wounded coyote.

And the lost mountain lion cub.

And the family of mice living in his backpack.

Yeah, he thought she didn't know about that one. At least the others he'd healed then released, or found a shifter parent for. He even had the audacity to snaffle pieces of her good cheese for the mice, like she wouldn't notice. As if.

A beak clicked by her ear. "Don't try that with me," she warned. "Caspian's the nice one."

"Oh, I don't know about that." Danny grinned as he emerged from the crush of people, dropping onto the bench beside her. He looked unusually relaxed and off-duty in his jeans and black t-shirt. "He just refused to give me his spare taco."

"It's spoken for," Caspian said dryly, pushing through after him. He offered the taco to the vulture with raised eyebrows. The bird lunged, beak snapping, and the three of them cringed as they watched the blur of meat and shredded lettuce.

"Naturally," Danny murmured, then turned back to Olivia. He dug his phone out of his pocket and offered it to her. "I got better footage. Look."

As far as Olivia could tell, it was still grainy as hell, the shapes on the screen more shadow than substance. But Danny stared down at his phone with a dreamy look on his face, so she nodded and clapped him on the shoulder.

"You'll get her, Danny."

"I don't want to *get* her. You make it sound like a hit." He stared for a second longer, then clicked the screen off, smirking up at them. "I just want to make contact. Check she's okay. It's my duty, you know. As a police officer."

"Funny, that." Caspian brushed taco shell crumbs off the bench and sat down on Olivia's other side. The vulture squawked and took off flapping, swooping clumsily to the nearest rooftop. A gargoyle tried to shoo it, then gave up, flipping Caspian off.

Olivia dropped her cheek onto his shoulder. His sculpted, manly shoulder. It still didn't feel real, somehow. He was like something out of her romance novels.

She wouldn't question it, she decided. Better to not go down that path. And besides, he wasn't perfect. Right this second, he had a slobbery fragment of the vulture's shredded lettuce stuck to his neck.

She peeled it off and flicked it towards the paving stones, the crowd surging with chatter and shouts of laughter. On the sidewalk, the Supernatural Airwaves van blared the radio from its speakers.

He wasn't perfect, but he was pretty damn close. And all she'd had to do was conjure him from oblivion.

THE END

Want more from Boiling River?

Check out the witch Delilah and her mysterious partner's love story, Hot as Hell—a novella in the Limited Edition Paranormal BBW anthology, Kiss of Magic. Available now in KU!

Read on for a sneak preview...

Teaser: Hot as Hell

"You knew about the demon."

Delilah stood, hands on hips, watching Wilhelmina stir a simmering pot in the kitchen. The smells wafting from the pot changed by the second—by turns garlicky and delicious, then light and floral, then fresh as peppermint. Delilah didn't want to know what her friend was cooking up. When it came to Will's potions, pleading ignorance was the best course.

"I saw no demon." A furtive smile tugged at Will's mouth.

"Well, he saw me. All of me." A blush crept over Delilah's cheeks, and she crossed her arms and raised her chin. She would not be embarrassed that some wandering demon saw her in her birthday suit. Not even when she remembered the deep velvet of his voice.

"My, my." Will smirked over her shoulder, stirring anticlockwise with the wooden spoon. "How deliciously wrong of him."

Delilah scoffed, resisting the urge to stamp her foot. She was a witch, damn it, not a sulky teenager.

"We can't encourage peepers, Wilhelmina." She only used her friend's full name when she was annoyed. "It'll scare off the other guests."

143

"Has he checked in, then?" Will asked lightly.

"Yes, I..." Delilah trailed off, her friend's words trickling through her brain. It was hard to think, this late at night, with her exhaustion piled heavy on her shoulders and Will's potion letting off that muddling steam. "What do you mean, has he checked in? He wasn't a guest?"

Will shrugged.

"That's even worse!" Delilah winced as her cry bounced off the copper saucepans hanging from the walls. She lowered her voice, hissing instead. "As a guest, he was a pervert. But as some lonely desert hobo—"

"He's in Room 13," Will interrupted. "If you'd like to have a word."

Her sentence was innocent enough, but the way she said it made Delilah want to poke her in the eye. Her tone dripped with suggestion and amusement, as though she saw straight through Delilah's cloud of denial, right through to her flustered, overheated insides.

Yes, the demon had a nice voice. Low and full of dark promise. And yes, he'd cut a striking figure in the dark, silhouetted against the night sky. But Delilah was trying to relax, damn it. Not get hot and bothered over some reprobate. Sneaking around in the desert like that, peeping at bathing witches.

"He can't stay here."

Will shrugged, the movement cascading through her draped satin shawls. "Alright. Go and kick him out."

"I will."

"Go on then."

"I intend to."

"So you say."

Delilah screwed her eyes shut, a headache pulsing in her

crown. She'd meant it earlier when she told Wilhelmina she was tired. Lately, she'd lashed on to her sanity with a fraying rope.

"Have a drink, first." Will's voice was soft. Conciliatory.

"I'm not going within three feet of that concoction."

"Not this. This is to scare off the skunks. Try the top shelf."

The witches prided themselves on their drinks collection, and they stashed their bottles high on a shelf in the kitchen. A step ladder was required to reach the drinks, even for the trolls who sometimes stayed, and they lured away the guests with easier pickings. Delilah crossed the kitchen, eyes still screwed shut, and grasped the ladder by memory. It bounced over the earthen tiles, its wood cracked and hollow, then wobbled as she placed it below the shelf.

She cracked one eye. The shelf was overhead, draped in cobwebs and half hidden in ivy. Bunches of dried chilies hung on either side, hot enough to make her lips sting when she stepped close on the ladder.

Tequila. Brandy. Stoppered, aged whisky. Wines gifted from fallen French kings; rum salvaged from shipwrecks.

Delilah clicked her tongue, then plucked off a bottle of elderflower gin, brewed by a Scottish hedge witch in the 1500s.

"Pour me one, too."

Delilah tossed a look over her shoulder.

"Lazy."

"I prefer 'skilled in the art of delegation.'"

She hid her grin, stepping back down the ladder and hunting down two crystal tumblers.

She'd confront the peeping demon. Toss him out on his ear. But first, she'd get good and drunk.

* * *

"Out!" Delilah rather liked the sound of her voice when she hollered. It was powerful. There was a ring to it. The demon's bedroom door bounced off his wall, and she marched inside Room 13. The floor tilted to one side, but she recovered seamlessly.

Yes. Gin had been a wonderful idea.

"Hello, Delilah." The demon strolled in from his balcony, his tunic unbuttoned to the navel. His abdomen was ridged with muscles, the skin smooth and golden, and his long legs ended in bare feet. "I missed you too."

Delilah held up a warning finger.

"That," she said, mustering her most disapproving tone, "is not why I'm here."

"Pity." A sinful smile curled the demon's mouth. His cheekbones were sharp enough to file her nails on. "Then how may I help you?"

It was… difficult. To throw him out when he was being so polite. It made her feel like the bad guy. Delilah sucked in a breath, throwing out her arms to steady herself when the room lurched again.

"You've been indulging, I see." The demon strolled closer.

"Why shouldn't I?" Delilah raised her chin, annoyed. Who was he to judge her, of all people? Demons had the worst self control.

"Not at all." His gaze raked over her from head to toe. "I thoroughly approve."

For some reason, that pissed her off more than his censure. She didn't want his approval, damn it—she didn't care an inch what he thought. Delilah rallied, balling her hands into fists

146

and propping them on her hips.

His eyes dropped to her generous curves, his expression hungry. Gods damn him, he was distracting.

"You need to leave." He raised his eyebrows, but she pushed on. "You're not welcome here."

"Have I done something wrong?" He cocked his head. "I've been a model guest so far."

"You watched me. In the springs."

He held up his palms. "I had no idea you'd be there. I'm a…" He trailed off, a smile tugging his mouth. "I'm a tourist. I was out for a stroll."

"In the desert," she said flatly. "With the scorpions and rattlesnakes. And the sinkholes and the trickster spirits."

The demon shrugged. "I've never been to a desert before."

"All the more reason to be careful!" Delilah pinched the bridge of her nose. She was getting off track. That gin was strong. "There are plenty of hotels in Boiling River. You'll have to go there."

"I can't." The demon flopped down on the bed, lounging like a male model. "I'm terribly injured."

He gestured to his foot. Delilah glanced down and let out a strangled cry at the bloody lump on the bed sheets. It was mauled, barely recognizable as a foot—but surely, when she came in—

"I'm so grateful for you letting me stay," he said smoothly, no ounce of pain in his voice. Delilah scowled at him, but what could she say? She couldn't send him back out into the desert with an injury like that, bastard or not.

"You conjured that."

The demon grinned. "Ouch," was all he said. He wiggled his bloody toes.

Delilah huffed out a breath and stomped back out of the room. He wanted to stay here? He wanted to fake an awful wound? Then he'd better brace himself for her herbal cure.

Her stinking, bone-throbbing, *ever* so effective cure.

* * *

Check out Hot as Hell now in the Kiss of Magic anthology!

Author's Note

Thank you for reading Ghost Track!

I hope you loved reading Caspian and Olivia's story as much as I loved writing it. I mean, who doesn't want a sexy ghost following them around? Patrick Swayze has a lot to answer for.

If you enjoyed this book, please consider leaving a review. They're super helpful for authors, they help other readers find new books to love, and they max out your Good Deed quota for the day.

Stay spooky!

Tabby xx

About the Author

Tabby Monroe writes quirky & creepy paranormal romance.

When she's not writing, Tabby can be found baking, hiking, and befriending local cats.

She lives on the Welsh coast with her very own gorgeous vamp.

You can connect with me on:
- 🌐 https://www.tabbymonroe.com
- 🔗 https://www.bookbub.com/authors/tabby-monroe
- 🔗 https://www.amazon.com/~/e/B08PDKSHB1

Subscribe to my newsletter:
- ✉ https://www.tabbymonroe.com/newsletter

www.ingramcontent.com/pod-product-compliance
Lightning Source LLC
Chambersburg PA
CBHW011435170626
46808CB00010B/3173

* 9 7 8 1 9 1 4 2 4 2 0 5 2 *